RAY BRADBURY'S "The Lost City of Mars"

The red planet's vast automated metropolis—abandoned countless centuries ago—bestirred itself to greet the visitors from Earth.

THEODORE STURGEON'S "One Foot and the Grave"

Her left foot wasn't a foot any more; it had become a cloven hoof, hairy-fetlocked, sharp and heavy. And his was even bigger and shaggier than hers!

CHAD OLIVER'S "The Marginal Man"

Twenty-nine light years from his home on Earth, the anthropologist stood in wonder and sadness on the edge of marvels, glimpsing a life beyond his understanding—a life he could never enter.

3 TO THE HIGHEST POWER

BRADBURY
OLIVER
STURGEON

AN AVON BOOK

This Avon edition is the first
publication in book form of the
novelets in *Three to the Highest Power*.

AVON BOOKS
A division of
The Hearst Corporation
959 Eighth Avenue
New York, New York 10019

First Avon Printing, February, 1968

AVON TRADEMARK REG. U.S. PAT. OFF. AND
FOREIGN COUNTRIES, REGISTERED TRADEMARK—
MARCA REGISTRADA, HECHO EN CHICAGO, U.S.A.

Printed in the U.S.A.

For ANTHONY BOUCHER,

who "discovered" Oliver,
promoted Bradbury and Sturgeon
and,
in eighty-seven splendidly edited issues
of **Fantasy and Science Fiction,**
perfected the Grand Art
of the Preface.

CONTENTS

3 TO THE HIGHEST POWER

RAY BRADBURY

Much has been written about him, just as he has written often of his own beginnings. We know he grew up in Waukegan, Illinois, as Ray Douglas Bradbury, a bespectacled, darkly imaginative boy, fascinated by the many-shelved town library, fearful of the ravine near his house, happy with his Aunt Neva (who read Poe to him) and his Uncle Einar (the man he fictionally transformed into a winged vampire), in love with Oz and Tarzan and Buck Rogers and summer night porches and Saturday matinees. We know about the lake near his town and of the black-tented October carnivals on the shore, about the top-hatted magicians who intrigued him, about his amateur magic acts and radio readings —and about his formative days as a frantic science fiction enthusiast in California, when he contributed to a dozen fan magazines and dreamed of rockets. It is well known, also, that he wrote his first novel at twelve, as a sequel to Burroughs, on a toy typewriter, that he sold newspapers on a corner for three years to support his fumbling, ill-starred early efforts at the short story, that he made his first sale just a month short of his twenty-first birthday, that he burned over a million bad words before beginning to write the good ones.

He exists today, a vitally alive man of forty-seven, straddling past and future, a spaceman in a straw hat with bicycle clips on his legs. The vanilla summers of a green, tree-shaded boyhood haunt his work; the red flare of a yet-uncharted Mars fires his mind. His stories —poetic, symbolic, passionate, evocative—reflect this

11

double self: parables of the future echoing his own yesterdays.

"Quite often," Ray admits, "the people in my Illinois stories cross-pollinate the people in my Martian stories, and I find whole families from 1928 showing up in the year 2000 and helping to colonize Mars."

Thus, the initial entry in his Martian series, "The Million-Year Picnic" (published in 1946), finds a typical midwestern family having their "outing" on Mars. In "The Strawberry Window" a homesick colonist imports stained glass windows and porch rockers from Earth. In the startling, much-reprinted "Mars Is Heaven" the spacemen of a rocket age land to confront a Victorian town. And Poe's *House of Usher* is reburned on the Red Planet, horrors and all, in Bradbury's "Usher II."

He sees no basic conflict here. "A man cannot possibly speak futures unless he has a strong sense of the past," Bradbury declares. "Thirty some years ago, at L.A. High, I was the only boy in my class who really believed in the Space Age, who believed we'd go off someday in rockets and land on Mars."

The genesis of Bradbury's Martian series can be traced directly back to this period, to 1940, when he printed his own fan magazine and included in it his story, "The Piper." Here, clearly, we find the roots of the mature fiction he would later write and collect into book form as *The Martian Chronicles*, and which would finally extend into 1967 and "The Lost City of Mars."

A few lines from this early effort reflect the mood and tone later adopted for the *Chronicles*: "Mars is a dying world . . ." [the old one said. "We] were once a brilliant race. Now, out there beyond the mountains, beyond the dead sea bottoms . . . the men from Earth . . . rip open the bowels of our planet, dig out our precious life blood . . . no culture, no art, no purpose . . . greedy, hopeless Earthlings . . . despoilers . . . Death for the men of Earth!"

In 1963, when Time, Inc. published a special Reading Program edition of *The Martian Chronicles*, they dubbed it "the finest creation of the best contemporary writer of science fiction." This Time, Inc. volume contained seventeen stories from the series, plus "bridge passages," with Bradbury's addition of "The Wilderness" and "The Fire Balloons," neither of which was in the original 1950 Doubleday book. (In all, Ray has penned thirty Martian tales, including "Christmas on Mars," sold to *Esquire,* but never printed.)

"Science fiction is the ideal literary form in which to express the demands of our age," Bradbury says. "We are a science-fictional people living in a science-fictional culture. . . . In this time of the rocket, man has a chance to be immortal. Man can seed the universe and live forever! People often say, 'How great it would have been to be alive when Columbus sailed!' But this is *just* that kind of time, with our sailing ships poised on the rim of a vast star wilderness. Our exciting, awesome voyage into space, to the moon and Mars and beyond, makes this the greatest age in all of man's history."

With more than four hundred stories, articles, essays, plays, and poems to his credit, Ray Bradbury is unique. He is not a technical man. Science baffles him (even as *Life* sends him chasing after astronauts and radar eyes); he can overemotionalize; he writes, more often than not, of symbols in place of flesh-and-blood characters. Yet, with all of his flaws he has combined his very considerable strengths, and has become (as Kingsley Amis calls him) "the Louis Armstrong of science fiction, the most widely-known, widely-read writer in the field." At its best, Bradbury's work glitters on a page; his prose touches the core of loneliness, of wonder and warmth. He communicates on a basic level, using subtle skills acquired over long years. It is impossible to overemphasize the humanizing influence his work has exerted on science fiction. Had he done nothing more than *The Martian Chronicles* his place would be secure.

I've known Ray since 1950, and whenever we meet he is invariably excited about something. Angry or delighted or disturbed, he is seldom placid; life holds great fascination and constant challenge for him. He fights for rapid transit, for the downtown library, for more open park areas within the city; he organizes classic film showings, serves on Writers' Guild committees, produces his own plays; he lectures at U.C.L.A., at Cal Tech, at L.A. State, at PTA meetings ("I'm the purest kind of hambone. In my teens I did a great deal of amateur acting and this is still an important part of my psyche."); he fires off letters to magazines and newspapers, prowls downtown bookshops, rides his bike in Venice, collects modern art, is involved in oil painting and animation and old radio shows (lovingly gathering discs of *Vic and Sade*); he vigorously defends Southern California against cultural attack; he writes poetry and light opera, delights in Disneyland, and stands shaken to watch 200,000-pound-thrust rockets fire up from Rocketdyne test pads. He loves his family, holds fast to his friends, works happily in his cellar, surrounded by jammed filing cabinets, his collection of Mexican masks, trunks of old comic strips from his childhood. He is the fulfilled man-boy, loved and loving.

Critic Gilbert Highet credits this talent and energy which "have transformed him from an eager, self-taught tale spinner into a distinguished American author."

Indeed, accolades and awards, medals and grants have come his way steadily since 1946 when his uniquely styled fiction began to gain solid recognition. (That year marked his first appearance in *Best American Short Stories*.)

Ray has written in several fields: crime and suspense, stories of Hollywood and of Europe, tales of Ireland (based on his six-month screen writing stint there with John Huston on *Moby Dick*), but he always returns to science fiction, since his visionary imagination is best served by the field which nurtured him.

"I want to sell people on the inevitability and the beauty and the distinction of the Space Age," he says. "The real job of a writer is to measure the difference between things as they are and things as they should be. That's the measuring stick imaginative writers over five thousand years have used: the dream of man, the disillusionment, the reality, these things that are con-

stantly moving in a circle through our consciousness.
. . . The future rushes upon us. To read the symbols it
writes on space with some prescience is our everlasting, frightening and exhilarating job."

"The Lost City of Mars" is the first new piece of
Martian fiction Bradbury has published since 1954; it
is also one of his most sustained efforts—since the
majority of Ray's stories are well below novelet length.
It is part of the basic fabric of *The Martian Chronicles*
and was written in conjunction with a projected screen
version of the book.

Ray Bradbury may take us to Illinois, 1928, or to
Mexico for the Day of the Dead, or to an Irish pub in
Dublin—but his final drive is to the stars, to red Mars
floating in a dark sea of space. Now, after fourteen
years, he revisits it.

The return trip is well worth taking.

THE LOST CITY OF MARS
Ray Bradbury

The great eye floated in space. And behind the great eye somewhere hidden away within metal and machinery was a small eye that belonged to a man who looked and could not stop looking at all the multitudes of stars and the diminishings and growings of light a billion billion miles away.

The small eye closed with tiredness. Captain John Wilder stood holding to the telescopic devices that probed the Universe and at last murmured, "Which one?"

The astronomer with him said, "Take your pick."

"I wish it were that easy." Wilder opened his eyes. "What's the data on that last star?"

"Same size and reading as our sun. Planetary system, possible."

"Possible. Not certain. If we pick the wrong star, God help the people° we send on a two-hundred-year journey to find a planet that may not be there. No, God help me, for the final selection is mine, and I may well send myself on that journey. So, how can we be sure?"

"We can't. We just make the best guess, send our starship out and pray."

"You are not very encouraging. That's it. I'm tired."

Wilder touched a switch that shut up tight the greater eye, this rocket-powered space lens that stared cold upon the abyss, saw far too much and knew little, and now knew nothing. The rocket laboratory drifted sightless on an endless night.

"Home," said the captain. "Let's go home."

And the blind beggar-after-stars wheeled on a spread of fire and ran away.

The frontier cities on Mars looked very fine from above. Coming down for a landing, Wilder saw the neons among the blue hills and thought, we'll light some worlds a billion miles off, and the children of the people living under these lights this instant, we'll make them immortal. Very simply, if we succeed, they will live forever.

Live forever. The rocket landed. Live forever.

The wind that blew from the frontier town smelled of grease. An aluminum-toothed jukebox banged somewhere. A junk yard rusted beside the rocketport. Old newspapers danced on the windy tarmac.

Wilder, motionless at the top of the gantry elevator, suddenly wished not to move down. The lights suddenly had become people and not words that, huge in the mind, could be handled with elaborate ease.

He sighed. The freight of people was too heavy. The stars were too far away.

"Captain?" said someone behind him.

He stepped forward. The elevator gave way. They sank toward a very real land with real people in it, who were waiting for him to choose.

At midnight the telegram bin hissed and exploded out a message projectile. Wilder, at his desk, surrounded by tapes and computation cards, did not touch it for a long while. When at last he pulled the message out, he scanned it, rolled it in a tight ball, then uncrumpled the message and read again:

FINAL CANAL BEING FILLED TOMORROW WEEK. YOU ARE INVITED CANAL YACHT PARTY. DISTINGUISHED GUESTS. FOUR-DAY JOURNEY TO SEARCH FOR LOST CITY. KINDLY ACKNOWLEDGE.

I. V. AARONSON.

Wilder blinked, and laughed quietly. He crumpled

the paper again, but stopped, lifted the telephone and said:

"Telegram to I. V. Aaronson, Mars City I. Answer affirmative. No sane reason why, but still—affirmative."

And hung up the phone. To sit for a long while watching this night that shadowed all the whispering, ticking and motioning machines.

The dry canal waited.

It had been waiting twenty thousand years for nothing but dust to filter through in ghost tides.

Now, quite suddenly, it whispered.

And the whisper became a rush and wall-caroming glide of waters.

As if a vast machined fist had struck the rocks somewhere, clapped the air and cried "Miracle!," a wall of water came proud and high along the channels, and lay down in all the dry places of the canal and moved on toward ancient deserts of dry bone, surprising old wharves and lifting up the skeletons of boats abandoned countless centuries before when the water burnt away to nothing.

The tide turned a corner and lifted up a boat as fresh as the morning itself, with new-minted silver screws and brass pipings, and bright new Earth-sewn flags. The boat, suspended from the side of the canal, bore the name Aaronson I.

Inside the boat, a man with the same name smiled. Mr. Aaronson sat listening to the waters live under the boat.

And the sound of the water was cut across by the sound of a hovercraft, arriving, and a motor bike, arriving, and in the air, as if summoned with magical timing, drawn by the glimmer of tides in the old canal, a number of gadfly people flew over the hills on jet-pack machines and hung suspended as if doubting this collision of lives caused by one rich man.

Scowling up with a smile, the rich man called to his children, cried them in from the heat with offers of food and drink.

"Captain Wilder! Mr. Parkhill! Mr. Beaumont!"

Wilder set his hovercraft down.

Sam Parkhill discarded his motor bike, for he had seen the yacht and it was a new love.

"My God," cried Beaumont, the actor, part of the frieze of people in the sky dancing like bright bees on the wind. "I've timed my entrance wrong. I'm early. There's no audience!"

"I'll applaud you down!" shouted the old man, and did so, then added, "Mr. Aikens!"

"Aikens?" said Parkhill. "The big-game hunter?"

"None other!"

And Aikens dived down as if to seize them in his harrying claws. He fancied his resemblance to the hawk. He was finished and stropped like a razor by the swift life he had lived. Not an edge of him but cut the air as he fell, a strange plummeting vengeance upon people who had done nothing to him. In the moment before destruction, he pulled up on his jets and, gently screaming, simmered himself to touch the marble jetty. About his lean middle hung a rifle belt. His pockets bulged like those of a boy from the candy store. One guessed he was stashed with sweet bullets and rare bombs. In his hands, like an evil child, he held a weapon that looked like a bolt of lightning fallen straight from the clutch of Zeus, stamped, nevertheless: MADE IN U. S. A. His face was sun-blasted dark. His eyes were cool surprises in the sun-wrinkled flesh, all mint-blue-green crystal. He wore a white porcelain smile set in African sinews. The earth did not quite tremble as he landed.

"The lion prowls the land of Judah!" cried a voice from the heavens. "Now do behold the lambs driven forth to slaughter!"

"Oh, for God's sake, Harry, shut up!" said a woman's voice.

And two more kites fluttered their souls, their dread humanity, on the wind.

The rich man jubilated.

"Harry Harpwell!"

"Behold the angel of the Lord who comes with

Annunciations!" the man in the sky said, hovering. "And the Annunciation is—"

"He's drunk again," his wife supplied, flying ahead of him, not looking back.

"Megan Harpwell," said the rich man, like an entrepreneur introducing his troupe.

"The poet," said Wilder.

"And the poet's barracuda wife," muttered Parkhill.

"I am not drunk," the poet shouted down the wind. "I am simply *high*." And here he let loose such a deluge of laughter that those below almost raised their hands to ward off the avalanche.

Lowering himself, like a fat dragon kite, the poet, whose wife's mouth was now clamped shut, bumbled over the yacht. He made the motions of blessing, and winked at Wilder and Parkhill.

"Harpwell," he called. "Isn't that a name to go with being a great modern poet who suffers in the present, lives in the past, steals bones from old dramatists' tombs, and flies on this new egg-beater wind-suck device, to call down sonnets on your head? I pity the old euphoric saints and angels who had no invisible wings like these so as to dart in oriole convolutions and ecstatic convulsions on the air as they sang their lines or damned souls to hell. Poor earthbound sparrows, wings clipped. Only their genius flew. Only their muse knew airsickness—"

"Harry," said his wife, her feet on the ground, eyes shut.

"Hunter!" called the poet. "Aikens! Here's the greatest game in all the world, a poet on the wing. I bare my breast. Let fly your honeyed bee sting! Bring me, Icarus, down, if your gun be sunbeams kindled in one tube, let free in single forest fires that escalate the sky to turn tallow, mush, candlewick and lyre to mere tarbabe. Ready, aim, fire!"

The hunter, in good humor, raised his gun.

The poet, at this, laughed a mightier laugh and, literally, exposed his chest by tearing aside his shirt.

At which moment a quietness came along the canal rim.

A woman appeared, walking. Her maid walked behind her. There was no vehicle in sight, and it seemed almost as if they had wandered a long way out of the Martian hills and now stopped.

The very quietness of her entrance gave dignity and attention to Cara Corelli.

The poet shut up his lyric in the sky and landed.

The company all looked together at this actress who gazed back without seeing them. She was dressed in a black jump suit that was the same color as her dark hair. She walked like a woman who has spoken little in her life and now stood facing them with the same quietness, as if waiting for someone to move without being ordered. The wind blew her hair out and down over her shoulders. The paleness of her face was shocking. Her paleness, rather than her eyes, stared at them.

Then, without a word, she stepped down into the yacht and sat in the front of the craft, like a figurehead that knows its place and goes there.

The moment of silence was over.

Aaronson ran his finger down the printed guest list.

"An actor, a beautiful woman who happens to be an actress, a hunter, a poet, a poet's wife, a rocket captain, a former technician. All aboard!"

On the afterdeck of the huge craft, Aaronson spread forth his maps.

"Ladies, gentlemen," he said. "This is more than a four-day drinking bout, party, excursion. This is a search!"

He waited for their faces to light properly, and for them to glance from his eyes to the charts, and then said:

"We are seeking the fabled Lost City of Mars, once called Dia-Sao, the City of Doom. Something terrible about it. The inhabitants fled as from a plague. The City left empty. Still empty now, centuries later."

"We," said Captain Wilder, "have charted, mapped and cross-indexed every acre of land on Mars in the last fifteen years. You can't mislay a city the size of the one you speak of."

"True," said Aaronson, "you've mapped it from the

sky, from the land. But you have *not* charted it via water, for the canals have been empty until now! So we shall take the new waters that fill this last canal and go where the boats once went in the olden days, and see the very last new things that need to be seen on Mars." The rich man continued: "And somewhere on our traveling, as sure as the breath in our mouths, we shall find the most beautiful, the most fantastic, the most awful city in the history of this old world. And walk in that city and—who knows?—find the reason why the Martians ran screaming away from it, as the legend says, thousands of years ago."

Silence. Then:

"Bravo! Well done." The poet shook the old man's hand.

"And in that city," said Aikens, the hunter, "mightn't there be weapons the like of which we've never seen?"

"Most likely, sir."

"Well." The hunter cradled his bolt of lightning. "I was bored of Earth, shot every animal, ran fresh out of beasts, and came here looking for newer, better, more dangerous man-eaters of any size or shape. Plus, now, new weapons! What more can one ask?"

And he dropped his blue-silver lightning bolt over the side. It sank in the clear water, bubbling.

"Let's get the hell out of here."

"Let us, indeed," said Aaronson, "get the good hell out."

And he pressed the button that launched the yacht.

And the water flowed the yacht away.

And the yacht went in the direction toward which Cara Corelli's quiet paleness was pointed: beyond.

The poet opened the first champagne bottle. The cork banged. Only the hunter did not jump.

The yacht sailed steadily through the day into night. They found an ancient ruin and had dinner there and a good wine imported 100,000,000 miles from Earth. It was noted that it had traveled well.

With the wine came the poet, and after quite a bit of the poet came sleep on board the yacht that moved away in search of a city that would not as yet be found.

At three in the morning, restless, unaccustomed to the gravity of a planet pulling at all of his body and not freeing him to dream, Wilder came out on the afterdeck of the yacht and found the actress there.

She was watching the waters slip by in dark revelations and discardments of stars.

He sat beside her and thought a question.

Just as silently, Cara Corelli asked herself the same question, and answered it.

"I am here on Mars because not long ago for the first time in my life, a man told me the truth."

Perhaps she expected surprise. Wilder said nothing. The boat moved as on a stream of soundless oil.

"I am a beautiful woman. I have been beautiful all of my life. Which means that from the start people lied because they simply wished to be with me. I grew up surrounded by the untruths of men, women and children who could not risk my displeasure. When beauty pouts, the world trembles.

"Have you ever seen a beautiful woman surrounded by men, seen them nodding, nodding? Heard their laughter? Men will laugh at anything a beautiful woman says. Hate themselves, yes, but they will laugh, say no for yes and yes for no.

"Well, that's how it was every day of every year for me. A crowd of liars stood between me and anything unpleasant. Their words dressed me in silks.

"But quite suddenly, oh, no more than six weeks ago, this man told me a truth. It was a small thing. I don't remember now what it was he said. But he didn't laugh. He didn't even smile.

"And no sooner was it out and over, the words spoken, than I knew a terrible thing had happened.

"I was growing old."

The yacht rocked gently on the tide.

"Oh, there would be more men who would, lying, smile again at what I said. But I saw the years ahead, when beauty could no longer stomp its small foot, and shake down earthquakes, make cowardice a custom among otherwise good men.

"The man? He took back his truth immediately, when he saw that he had shocked me. But it was too late. I bought a one-way fare to Mars. Aaronson's invitation, when I arrived, put me on this new journey that will end . . . who knows where."

Wilder found that during this last he had reached out and taken her hand.

"No," she said, withdrawing. "No word. No touch. No pity. No self-pity." She smiled for the first time. "Isn't it strange? I always thought, wouldn't it be nice, someday, to hear the truth, to give up the masquerade? How wrong I was. It's no fun at all."

She sat and watched the black waters pour by the boat. When she thought to look again, some while later, the seat beside her was empty. Wilder was gone.

On the second day, letting the new waters take them where it wished to go, they sailed toward a high range of mountains and lunched, on the way, in an old shrine, and had dinner that night in a further ruin. The Lost City was not much talked about. They were sure it would never be found.

But on the third day, without anyone's saying, they felt the approach of a great presence.

It was the poet who finally put it in words.

"Is God humming under His breath somewhere?"

"What a fierce scum you are," said his wife. "Can't you speak plain English even when you gossip?"

"Dammit, listen!" cried the poet.

So they listened.

"Don't you feel as if you stood on the threshold of a giant blast-furnace kitchen and inside somewhere, all comfortably warm, vast hands, flour-gloved, smelling of wondrous tripes and miraculous viscera, bloodied and proud of the blood, somewhere God cooks out the dinnertime of life? In that caldron sun, a brew to make the flowering forth of life on Venus, in that vat, a stew broth of bones and nervous heart to run in animals on planets ten billion light-years gone. And isn't God content at His fabulous workings in the great kitchen Universe, where He has menu'd out a

history of feasts, famines, deaths and reburgeonings for
a billion billion years? And if God be content, would
He not hum under His breath? Feel your bones. Aren't
the marrows teeming with that hum? For that matter,
God not only hums, He sings in the elements. He
dances in molecules. Eternal celebration swarms us.
Something is near. Sh."

He pressed his fat finger to his pouting lips.

And now all were silent, and Cara Corelli's paleness
searchlighted the darkening waters ahead.

They all felt it. Wilder did. Parkhill did. They
smoked to cover it. They put the smokes out. They
waited in the dusk.

And the humming grew nearer. And the hunter,
smelling it, went to join the silent actress at the bow
of the yacht. And the poet sat to write down the words
he had spoken.

"Yes," he said, as the stars came out. "It's almost
upon us. It has . . ." he took a breath, ". . . arrived."

The yacht passed into a tunnel.

The tunnel went under a mountain.

And the City was there.

It was a city within a hollow mountain with its own
meadows surrounding it and its own strangely colored
and illumined stone sky above it. And it had been lost
and remained lost for the simple reason that people
had tried flying to discover it or had unraveled roads
to find it, when all the while the canals that led to it
stood waiting for simple walkers to tread where once
waters had trod.

And now the yacht filled with strange people from
another planet touched an ancient wharf.

And the City stirred.

In the old days, cities were alive or dead if there
were not people in them. It was that simple. But in the
later days of life on Earth or Mars, cities did not die.
They slept. And in their dreamful coggeries and en-
wheeled slumbers they remembered how once it was or
how it might be again.

So as, one by one, the party filed out on the dock,

they felt a great personage, the hidden, oiled, the metaled and shining soul of the metropolis slide in a landfall of muted and hidden fireworks toward becoming fully awake.

The weight of the new people on the dock caused a machined exhalation. They felt themselves on a delicate scale. The dock sank a millionth of an inch.

And the City, the cumbrous Sleeping Beauty of a nightmare device, sensed this touch, this kiss, and slept no more.

Thunder.

In a wall a hundred feet high stood a gate seventy feet wide. This gate, in two parts, now rumbled back, to hide within the wall.

Aaronson stepped forward.

Wilder moved to intercept him. Aaronson sighed.

"Captain, no advice, please. No warnings. No patrols going on ahead to flush out villains. The City wants us in. It welcomes us. Surely you don't imagine anything's *alive* in there? It's a robot place. And don't look as if you think it's a time bomb. It hasn't seen fun and games in—what? Do you read Martian hieroglyphs? That cornerstone. The City was built at least twenty thousand years ago."

"And abandoned," said Wilder.

"You make it sound like a plague drove them—"

"Not a plague." Wilder stirred uneasily, feeling himself weighed on the great scales beneath his feet. "Something. Something . . ."

"Let's find out! In, all of you!"

Singly, and in pairs, the people from Earth stepped over the threshold.

Wilder, last of all, stepped across.

And the City came more alive.

The metal roofs of the City sprang wide like the petals of a flower.

Windows flicked wide like the lids of vast eyes to stare down upon them.

A river of sidewalks gently purled and washed at their feet, machined creekways that gleamed off through the City.

Aaronson gazed at the metal tides with pleasure. "Well, by God, the burden's off me! I was going to picnic you all. But that's the City's business now. Meet you back here in two hours to compare notes! Here goes!"

And saying this, he leaped out onto the scurrying silver carpet that treaded him swiftly away.

Wilder, alarmed, moved to follow. But Aaronson cried jovially back:

"Come on in, the water's fine!"

And the metal river whisked him, waving, off.

And one by one they stepped forward and the moving sidewalk drifted them away. Parkhill, the hunter, the poet and his wife, the actor, and then the beautiful woman and her maid. They floated like statues mysteriously borne on volcanic fluids that swept them anywhere, or nowhere, they could only guess.

Wilder jumped. The river seized his boots gently. Following, he went away into the avenues and around the bends of parks and through fiords of buildings.

And behind them, the dock and the gate stood empty. There was no trace to show they had arrived. It was almost as if they had never been.

Beaumont, the actor, was the first to leave the traveling pathway. A certain building caught his eye. And the next thing he knew, he had leaped off and edged near, sniffing.

He smiled.

For now he knew what kind of building he stood before, because of the odor that drifted from it.

"Brass polish. And, by God, that means only one thing!"

Theater.

Brass doors, brass rails, brass rings on velvet curtains.

He opened the door of the building and stepped in. He sniffed and laughed aloud. Yes. Without a sign or a light, the smell alone, the special chemistry of metals and dust torn free of a million tickets.

And above all . . . he listened. The silence.

"The silence that waits. No other silence in the

world waits. Only in a theater will you find that. The
very particles of air chafe themselves in readiness. The
shadows sit back and hold their breath. Well . . . ready
or not . . . here I come . . ."

The lobby was green velvet undersea.

The theater itself: red velvet undersea, only dimly
perceived as he opened the double doors. Somewhere
beyond was a stage.

Something shuddered like a great beast. His breath
had dreamed it alive. The air from his half-opened
mouth caused the curtains a hundred feet away to softly furl and unfurl in darkness like all-covering wings.

Hesitantly, he took a step.

A light began to appear in a high ceiling where a
school of miraculous prism fish swam upon themselves.

The oceanarium light played everywhere. He gasped.

A thousand people sat motionless in the false dusk.
True, they were small, fragile, rather dark, they wore
silver masks, yet—people!

He knew, without asking, they had sat here for endless centuries.

Yet they were not dead.

They were—he reached out a hand. He tapped the
wrist of a man seated on the aisle.

The hand tinkled quietly.

He touched the shoulder of a woman. She chimed.
Like a bell.

Yes, they had waited some few thousand years. But
then, machines have a property of waiting.

He took a further step and froze.

For a sigh had passed over the crowd.

It was like the sound, the first small sound a newborn babe must make in the moment before it really
sucks, bleats and shocks out its wailing surprise at being
alive.

A thousand such sighs faded in the velvet portieres.

Beneath the masks, hadn't a thousand mouths drifted
ajar?

He moved. He stopped.

Two thousand eyes blinked wide in the velvet dusk.
He moved again.

A thousand silent heads wheeled on their ancient but well-oiled cogs.

They looked at him.

An unquenchable cold ran wild in him.

He turned to run.

But their eyes would not let him go.

And, from the orchestra pit: music.

He looked and saw, slowly rising, an insect agglomeration of instruments, all strange, all grotesquely acrobatic in their configurations. These were being softly thrummed, piped, touched and massaged in tune.

The audience, with a motion, turned their gaze to the stage.

A light flashed on. The orchestra struck a grand fanfare chord.

The red curtains parted. A spotlight fixed itself to front center, blazing upon an empty dais where sat an empty chair.

Beaumont waited.

No actor appeared.

A stir. Several hands were lifted to left and right. The hands came together. They beat softly in applause.

Now the spotlight wandered off the stage and up the aisle.

The heads of the audience turned to follow the empty ghost of light. The masks glinted softly. The eyes behind the masks beckoned with warm color.

Beaumont stepped back.

But the light came steadily. It painted the floor with a blunt cone of pure whiteness.

And stopped, nibbling, at his feet.

The audience turned, applauded even louder now. The theater banged, roared, ricocheted with their ceaseless tide of approbation.

Everything dissolved within him, from cold to warm. He felt as if he had been thrust raw into a downpour of summer rain. The storm rinsed him with gratitude. His heart jumped in great compulsive beats. His fists let go of themselves. His skeleton relaxed. He waited a moment longer, with the rain drenching over his upthrust and thankful cheeks and hammering his hungry

eyelids so they fluttered to lock against themselves, and
then he felt himself, like a ghost on battlements, led by
a ghost light, lean, step, drift, move down and along
the incline, sliding to beautiful ruin, now no longer
walking but striding, not striding but in full-tilted run,
and the masks glittering, the eyes hot with delight and
fantastic welcoming, the flights of hands on the disturbed air in upflung dove-winged rifle-shot flight. He felt
the steps collide with his shoes. The applause slammed
to a shutdown.

He swallowed. Then slowly he ascended the steps
and stood in the full light with a thousand masks fixed
to him and two thousand eyes watchful, and he sat
in the empty chair, and the theater grew darker, and
the immense hearth-bellow breathing softer out of the
lyre-metal throats, and there was only the sound of a
mechanical beehive thrived with machinery musk in
the dark.

He held onto his knees. He let go. And at last he
spoke:

"To be or not to be—"

The silence was complete.

Not a cough. Not a stir. Not a rustle. Not a blink.
All waited. Perfection. The perfect audience. Perfect,
forever and forever. Perfect. Perfect.

He tossed his words slowly into that perfect pond
and felt the soundless ripples disperse and gentle away.

"—that is the question."

He talked. They listened. He knew that they would
never let him go now. They would beat him insensible
with applause. He would sleep a child's sleep and arise
to speak again. All of Shakespeare, all of Shaw, all of
Molière, every bit, crumb, lump, joint and piece. *Himself* in repertory!

He arose to finish.

Finished, he thought: Bury me! Cover me! Smother
me deep!

Obediently, the avalanche came down the mountain.

Cara Corelli found a palace of mirrors.
The maid remained outside.

And Cara Corelli went in.

As she walked through a maze, the mirrors took away a day, and then a week, and then a month and then a year and then two years of time from her face.

It was a palace of splendid and soothing lies. It was like being young once more. It was being surrounded by all those tall bright glass mirror men who would never again in your life tell you the truth.

Cara walked to the center of the palace. By the time she stopped, saw herself twenty-five years old, in every tall bright mirror face.

She sat down in the middle of the bright maze. She beamed around in happiness.

The maid waited outside for perhaps an hour. And then she went away.

This was a dark place with shapes and sizes as yet unseen. It smelled of lubricating oil, the blood of tyrant lizards with cogs and wheels for teeth, which lay strewn and silent in the dark, waiting.

A titan's door slowly gave a slithering roar, like a backswept armored tail, and Parkhill stood in the rich oily wind blowing out around him. He felt as if someone had pasted a white flower on his face. But is was only a sudden surprise of a smile.

His empty hands hung at his sides and they made impulsive and completely unconscious gestures forward. They beggared the air. So, paddling silently, he let himself be moved into the garage, machine shop, repair shed, whatever it was.

And filled with holy delight and a child's glee at what he beheld, he walked and slowly turned.

For as far as his eye could see stood vehicles.

Vehicles that ran on the earth. Vehicles that flew in the air. Vehicles that stood ready with wheels to go in any direction. Vehicles with two wheels. Vehicles with three or four or six or eight. Vehicles that looked like butterflies. Vehicles that resembled ancient motor bikes. Three thousand stood ranked here, four thousand glinted ready there. Another thousand were tilted over, wheels off, copper guts exposed, waiting to be repaired. Still another thousand were lifted high on spidery repair hoists, their lovely undersides revealed to view, their disks and tubes and coggeries all intricate and fine and needful of touching, unbolting, revalving, rewiring, oiling . . .

Parkhill's palms itched.

He walked forward through the primeval smell of swamp oils among the dead and waiting to be revived ancient but new armored mechanical reptiles, and the more he looked the more he ached his grin.

The City was a city all right, and, to a point, self-sustaining. But, eventually, the rarest butterflies of metal gossamer, gaseous oil and fiery dream sank to earth, the machines that repaired the machines that repaired the machines grew old, ill and damaging of themselves. Here then was the bestial garage, the slumberous elephant's bone yard where the aluminum dragons crawled rusting out their souls, hopeful of one live person left among so much active but dead metal, that person to put things right. One God of the machines to say, you Lazarus-elevator, rise up! You hovercraft, be reborn! And anoint them with leviathan oils, tap them with magical wrench and send them forth to almost eternal lives in and on the air and above the quicksilver paths.

Parkhill moved among nine hundred robot men and women slaughtered by simple corrosion. He would cure their rust.

Now. If he started now, thought Parkhill, rolling up his sleeves and staring off down a corridor of machines that ran waiting for a solid mile of garage, shed, hoist, lift, storage bin, oil tank and strewn shrapnel of tools glittering and ready for his grip; if he started now, he might work his way to the end of the giant's ever-constant garage, accident, collision and repair-works shed in thirty years!

A billion bolts to be tightened. A billion motors to be tinkered! A billion gross anatomical mysteries to lie under, a grand oil-dripped-upon orphan, alone, alone, alone with the always beautiful and never talking back hummingbird-commotion devices, accouterments and miraculous contraptions.

His hands weighed him toward the tools. He clutched a wrench. He found a forty-wheeled low running sled. He lay down on it. He sculled the garage in a long whistling ride. The sled scuttled.

Parkhill vanished beneath a great car of some ancient design.

Out of sight, you could hear him working on the gut of the machine. On his back, he talked up at it. And when he slapped it to life, at last, the machine talked back.

Always the silver pathways ran somewhere.

Thousands of years now they had run empty, carrying only dust to destinations away and away among the high and dreaming buildings.

Now, on one traveling path, Aaronson came borne like an aging statue.

And the more the road propelled him, the faster the City exposed itself to his view, the more buildings that passed, the more parks that sprang into sight, the more his smile faded. His color changed.

"Toy," he heard himself whisper. The whisper was ancient. "Just another," and here his voice grew so small it faded away, ". . . another toy."

A supertoy, yes. But his life was full of such and had always been so. If it was not some slot machine, it was the next-size dispenser or a jumbo-size hi-fi stereo speaker. From a lifetime of handling metallic sandpaper, he felt his arms rubbed away to a nub. Mere pips, his fingers. No, handless, and lacking wrists. Aaronson, the Seal Boy!!! His mindless flippers clapped applause to a city that was, in reality, no more and no less than an economy-size jukebox ravening under its idiot breath. And—he knew the tune! God help him. He *knew* the tune.

He blinked just once.

An inner eyelid came down like cold glass.

He turned and trod the silver waters of the path.

He found a moving river of steel to take him back toward the great gate itself.

On the way, he met Cara Corelli's maid, wandering lost on her own silver stream.

As for the poet and his wife, their running battle tore echoes everywhere. They cried down avenues, cracked panes in shops, battered leaves from seventy varieties of park bush and tree, and only ceased when drowned by a thundering fountain display they passed, like a rise of clear fireworks upon the metropolitan air.

"The whole thing is," said his wife, punctuating one of his dirtier responses, "you only came along so you could lay hands on the nearest woman and spray her ears with bad breath and worse poetry."

The poet muttered a foul word.

"You're worse than the actor," said his wife. "Always at it. Don't you ever shut up?"

"Don't you?" he cried. "Ah God, I've curdled inside. Shut up, woman, or I'll throw myself in the founts!"

"No. You haven't bathed in years. You're the pig of the century! Your picture should grace the *Swine Herder's Annual!*"

"That *did* it!"

Doors slammed on a building.

By the time she got off and ran back and fisted the doors, they were locked.

"Coward!" she shrieked. "Open up!"

A foul word came echoing out, dimly.

"Ah, listen to that sweet silence," he whispered, to himself, in the great shelled dark.

Harpwell found himself in a soothing hugeness, a vast womblike building, over which hung a canopy of pure serenity, a starless void.

In the middle of this room, which was roughly a two-hundred-foot circle, stood a device, a machine. In this machine were dials and rheostats and switches, a seat and a steering wheel.

"What kind of junk is this?" whispered the poet,

but edged near, and bent to touch. "Christ-off-the-cross and bearing mercy, it smells of what? Blood and mere guts? No, for it's clean as a virgin's frock. Still it does fill the nose. Violence. Simple destruction. I can feel the damn carcass tremble like a nervous highbred hound. It's full of *stuffs*. Let's try a swig."

He sat in the machine.

"What do I twig first? This?"

He snapped a switch.

The Baskerville-hound machine whimpered in its dog slumberings.

"Good beast." He flicked another switch. "How do you go, brute? When the damn device is in full tilt, where to? You lack wheels. Well, surprise me. I dare."

The machine shivered.

The machine bolted.

He held tight to the steering wheel.

"Holy God!"

For he was on a highway, racing fast.

Air sluiced by. The sky flashed over in running colors.

The speedometer read seventy, eighty.

And the highway ribboned away ahead, flashing toward him. Invisible wheels slapped and banged on an increasingly rough road.

Far away, ahead, a car appeared.

It was running fast. And—

"It's on the wrong side of the road! Do you see that, wife? The wrong side."

Then he realized his wife was not here.

He was alone in a car racing—ninety miles an hour now—toward another car racing at a similar speed.

He veered the wheel.

His vehicle moved to the left.

Almost instantly, the other car did a compensating move and ran back over to the left.

"The damn fool, what does he think—where's the blasted brake?"

He stomped the floor. There was no brake. Here was a strange machine indeed. One that ran as fast as you wished, but never stopped until what? it ran itself down? There was no brake. Nothing but—further accelerators. A whole series of round buttons on the floor, which as he tromped them, surged power into the motor.

Ninety, a hundred, a hundred and twenty miles an hour.

"God in heaven!" he screamed. "We're going to hit! How do you like that, girl?"

And in the last instant before collision, he imagined she rather liked it fine.

The cars hit. They erupted in gaseous flame. They burst apart in flinders. They tumbled. He felt himself jerked now this way, now that. He was a torch hurtled skyward. His arms and legs danced a crazy rigadoon in mid-air as he felt his peppermint-stick bones snap in brittle and agonizing ecstasies. Then, clutching death, as a dark mate, gesticulating, he fell away in a black surprise, drifting toward further nothings.

He lay dead.

He lay dead a long while.

Then he opened one eye.

He felt the slow burner under his soul. He felt the bubbled water rising to the top of his mind like tea brewing.

"I'm dead," he said, "but alive. Did you see all that, wife? Dead but alive."

He found himself sitting in the vehicle, upright.

He sat there for ten minutes thinking about all that had happened.

"Well now," he mused. "Was that not interesting? Not to say fascinating? Not to say almost exhilarating? I mean, sure, it knocked the stuff out of me, scared the soul out one ear and back the other, hit my wind and tore my seams, broke the bones and shook the wits, but, but, but, wife, but, but, but, dear sweet Meg, Meggy, Megeen, I wish you were here, it might tamp the tobacco tars out of your half-ass lungs and bray the mossy graveyard backbreaking meanness from your marrow. Let me see here now, wife, let's have a look, Harpwell-my-husband-the-poet."

He tinkered with the dials.

He thrummed the great hound motor.

"Shall we chance another diversion? Try another embattled picnic excursion? Let's."

And he set the car on its way.

Almost immediately, the vehicle was traveling a hundred and then a hundred and fifty miles per hour.

Almost immediately, an opposing car appeared ahead on the wrong side of the road.

"Death," said the poet. "Are you always here, then? Do you hang about? Is this your questing place? Let's test your mettle!"

The car raced. The opposing car hurtled.

He wheeled over into the far left lane.

The opposing car shifted, homing toward Destroy.

"Yes, I see, well, then, this," said the poet.

And switched a switch and jumped another throttle.

In the instant before impact, the two cars transformed themselves, shuttering through illusory veils, they became jetcraft at take-off. Shrieking, the two jets banged flame, tore air, yammered back sound-barrier explosions before the mightiest one of all—as the two bullets impacted, fused, interwove, interlaced blood, mind and eternal blackness, and fell away into a net of strange and peaceful midnight.

I'm dead, he thought again.

And it feels fine, thanks.

He awoke at the touch of his own smile.

He was seated in the vehicle.

Twice dead, he thought, and feeling better each time. Why? isn't that odd? Curiouser and curiouser. Queer beyond queerness.

He thrummed the motor again.

What this time?

Does it locomote? he wondered. How about a big black choo-choo train out of half-primordial times.

And he was on his way, an engineer. The sky flicked over with swift illusions of pouring smoke and steaming whistle and huge wheel within wheel on grinding track, and the track ahead wound through hills, and far on up around a mountain came another train, black as a buffalo herd, pouring belches of smoke, on the same two rails, the same track, heading toward wondrous accident.

"I see," said the poet. "I do begin to see. I begin to know what this is used for; for the poor wandering idiots of a world, confused, and sore put upon by mothers as soon as dropped from wombs, insulted with Christian guilt, and gone mad from the need of destruction, and collecting a pittance of hurt here and scar tissue there, and a larger portable wife grievance beyond, but one thing sure, we do want to die, we do want to be killed, and here's the very thing for it, in convenient quick pay! So pay it out, machine, dole it out, sweet raving device! Rape away, death! I'm your very man."

And the two locomotives met and climbed each other. Up a black ladder of explosion they wheeled and locked their drive shafts and plastered their slick Negro bellies together and rubbed boilers and beautifully banged the night in a single outflung whirl and flurry of meteor and flame. Then the locomotives, in a cumbrous rapine dance, seized and melted together with their violence and passion, gave a monstrous curtsy and fell off the mountain and took a thousand years to go all the way down to the rocky pits.

The poet awoke and immediately grabbed the controls. He was humming under his breath, stunned. He was singing wild tunes. His eyes flashed. His heart beat more swiftly.

"More, more, I see it now, I know what to do, more more, please, O God, more, for the truth shall set me free, more!"

He hoofed three, four, five pedals.

He snapped six switches.

The vehicle was auto-jet-locomotive-glider-missile-rocket.

He ran, he steamed, he roared, he soared, he flew. Cars veered toward him. Locomotives loomed. Jets rammed. Rockets screamed.

And in one wild three-hour spree he hit two hundred cars, rammed twenty trains, blew up ten gliders, exploded forty missiles, and, far out in space, gave up his glorious soul in a final Fourth of July death celebration as an interplanetary rocket going two hundred thousand miles an hour struck an iron planetoid and went beautifully to hell.

In all, in a few short hours he figured he must have been torn apart and put back together a few times less than five hundred.

When it was all over, he sat not touching the wheel, his feet free of the pedals.

After a half hour of sitting there, he began to laugh. He threw his head back and let out great war whoops. Then he got up, shaking his head, drunker than ever in his life, really drunk now, and he knew he would stay that way forever, and never need drink again.

I'm punished, he thought, really punished at last. Really hurt at last, and hurt enough, over and over, so I will never need hurt again, never need to be destroyed again, never have to collect another insult or take another wound, or ask for a simple grievance. God bless the genius of man and the inventors of such machines, that enable the guilty to pay and at last be rid of the dark albatross and the awful burden. Thank you, City, thank you, old blueprinter of needful souls. Thank you. And which way out?

A door slid open.

His wife stood waiting for him.

"Well, there you are," she said. "And still drunk."

"No," he said. "Dead."

"Drunk."

"Dead," he said, "beautifully dead at last. Which means, free. I won't need you anymore, dead Meg-Meggy-Megeen. You're set free, also, like an awful conscience. Go haunt someone else, girl. Go destroy. I forgive you your sins on me, for I have at last forgiven myself. I am off the Christian hook. I am the dear wandering dead who, dead, can at last live. Go and do likewise, lady. Inside with you. Be punished and set free. So long, Meg. Farewell. Toodle-oo."

He wandered away.

"Where do you think you're going?" she cried.

"Why, out into life and the blood of life, and happy at last."

"Come back here!" she screamed.

"You can't stop the dead, for they wander the Universe, happy as children in the dark field."

"Harpwell!" she brayed. "Harpwell!"

But he stepped on a river of silver metal.

And let the river bear him laughing until the tears glittered on his cheeks, away and away from the shriek and the bray and the scream of that woman, what was her name? no matter, back there, and gone.

And when he reached the gate he walked out and along the canal in the fine day, heading toward the far towns.

By that time, he was singing every old tune he had known as a child of six . . .

Behind him, by the strange building that had set him free, his wife stood a long while staring at the metal path that had floated him away. Then slowly she turned to glare at the enemy building. She fisted the door once. It slid open, waiting. She sniffed. She scowled at the interior.

Then, steadily, hands ready to seize and grapple, she advanced. With each step she grew bolder. Her face thrust like an ax at the strange air.

Behind her, unnoticed, the door closed.

It did not open again.

It was a church.

It was not a church.

Wilder let the door swing shut.

He stood in cathedral darkness, waiting.

The roof, if roof there was, breathed up a great suspense, flowed up beyond reach or sight.

The floor, if floor there was, was a mere firmness beneath. It, too, was black.

And then the stars came out. It was like that first night of childhood when his father had taken him out beyond the city to a hill where the streetlights could not diminish the Universe. And there were a thousand, no ten thousand, no ten million billion stars filling the darkness. The stars were manifold and bright, and they did not care. Even then he had known: They do not care. If I breathe or do not breathe, live or die, the eyes that look from all around don't care. And he had seized his father's hand and gripped tight, as if he might fall up into that abyss.

Now, in this building, he was full of the old terror and the old sense of beauty and the old silent crying out after mankind. The stars filled him with pity for small men lost in so much size.

Then yet another thing happened.

Beneath his feet, space opened wide and let through yet another billion sparks of light.

He was suspended as a fly is held upon a vast telescopic lens. He walked on a water of space. He stood upon a transparent flex of great eye, and all about him, as on a night in winter, beneath foot and above head, in all directions, were nothing but stars.

So, in the end, it was a church, it was a cathedral, a multitude of far-flung universal shrines, here a worshiping of Horsehead Nebula, there Orion's galaxy, and there Andromeda, like the head of God, fiercely gazed and thrust through the raw dark stuffs of night to stab his soul and pin it writhing against the backside of his flesh.

God, everywhere, fixed him with shutterless and unblinking eyes.

And he, a bacterial shard of that same Flesh, stared back and winced but the slightest.

He waited. And a planet drifted upon the void. It spun by once with a great mellow autumn face. It circled and came under him.

And he stood upon a far world of green grass and great lush trees, where the air was fresh, and a river ran by like the rivers of childhood, flashing the sun and leaping with fish.

He knew that he had traveled very far to reach this world. Behind him lay the rocket. Behind lay a century of travel, of sleeping, of waiting, and now, here was the reward.

"Mine?" he asked the simple air, the simple grass, the long simplicity of water that spilled by in the shallow sands.

And the world answered wordless: Yours.

Yours without the long travel and the boredom, yours without ninety-nine years of flight from Earth, of sleeping in kept tubes, of intravenous feedings, of nightmares dreamed of Earth lost and gone, yours without torture, without pain, yours without trial and error, failure and destruction. Yours without sweat and terror. Yours without a falling down of tears. Yours. Yours.

But Wilder did not put out his hands to accept.

And the sun dimmed in the alien sky.

And the world drifted from under his feet.

And yet another world swam up and passed in a huge parade of even brighter glories.

And this world, too, spun up to take his weight. And here, if anything, the fields were richer green, the mountains capped with melting snows, far fields ripening with strange harvests, and scythes waiting on the edge of fields for him to lift and sweep and cut the grain and live out his life any way that he might.

Yours. The merest touch of weather upon the hairs within his ear said this. Yours.

And Wilder, without shaking his head, moved back. He did not say no. He thought his rejection.

And the grass died in the fields.

The mountains crumbled.

The river shallows ran to dust.

And the world sprang away.

And Wilder stood again in space where God had stood before creating a world out of chaos.

And at last he spoke and said to himself:

"It would be easy. Oh Lord, yes, I'd like that. No work, nothing, just accept. But . . . You can't *give* me what I want."

He looked at the stars.

"Nothing can be given, ever."

The stars were growing dim.

"It's really very simple. I must borrow, I must earn. I must take."

The stars quivered and died.

"Much obliged and thank you, no."

The stars were all gone.

He turned and, without looking back, walked upon darkness. He hit the door with his palm. He strode out into the City.

He refused to hear if the machine Universe behind him cried out in a great chorus, all cries and wounds, like a woman scorned. The crockery in a vast robot kitchen fell. By the time it hit the floor, he was gone.

It was a museum of weapons.

The hunter walked among the cases.

He opened a case and hefted a weapon constructed like a spider's antennae.

It hummed, and a flight of metal bees sizzled out the rifle bore, flew and stung a target-mannequin some yards away, then fell lifeless, clattering to the floor.

The hunter nodded with admiration, and put the rifle back in the case.

He prowled on, curious as a child, testing yet other weapons here and there that dissolved glass or caused metal to run in bright yellow pools of molten lava.

"Excellent! Absolutely great!"

His cry rang out again and again as he slammed cases open and shut, and finally chose the gun.

It was a gun that, without fuss or fury, did away with matter. You pressed the button, there was a brief discharge of blue light and the target simply vanished. No blood. No bright lava. No trace.

"All right," he announced, leaving the place of guns, "we have the weapon. How about the game, the grandest beast ever in the long hunt?"

He leaped onto the moving sidewalk.

An hour later he had passed a thousand buildings and scanned a thousand open parks without itching his finger.

He moved uneasily from treadway to treadway, shifting speeds now in this direction, now in that.

Until at last he saw a river of metal that sped underground.

Instinctively, he jumped toward that.

The metal stream carried him down into the secret gut of the City.

Here all was warm blood darkness. Here strange pumps moved the pulse of the City. Here were distilled the sweats that lubricated the roadways and lifted the elevators and swarmed the offices and stores with motion.

The hunter half crouched on the roadway. His eyes squinted. Perspiration gathered in his palms. His trigger finger greased the metal gun, sliding.

"Yes," he whispered. "By God, now. This is it. The City itself . . . the great beast. Why didn't I think of that? The animal City, the dread carnivore that has men for breakfast, lunch and dinner, it kills them with machines, it munches their bones like bread sticks, it spits them out like toothpicks, and it lives long after they die. The City, by God, the City. Well now . . ."

He glided through dark grottoes of television eyes that showed him remote parkways and high towers.

Deeper within the belly of the underground world he sank as the river lowered itself. He passed a school of computers that chattered in maniac chorus. He shuddered as a cloud of paper confetti from one titan machine, holes punched out to perhaps record his passing, fell upon him in a whispered snow.

He raised his gun. He fired.

The machine disappeared.

He fired again. A skeleton strutwork under yet another machine vanished.

The City screamed.

At first very low and then very high, then rising, falling, like a siren. Lights flashed. Bells began to ricochet alarms. The metal river shuddered under his feet. He fired at television screens that glared all white upon him. They blinked out and did not exist.

The City screamed higher until he raved against it, himself.

He did not see, until it was too late, that the road on which he sped fell into the gnashing maw of a machine that was used for some purpose long forgotten centuries before.

He thought that by pressing the trigger he would make the terrible mouth disappear. It did indeed vanish. But as the roadway sped on and he whirled and fell as it picked up speed, he realized at last that his weapon did not truly destroy, it merely made invisible what was there and what still remained, though unseen.

He gave a terrible cry to match the cry of the City. He flung out the gun in a last blow. The gun went into cogs and wheels and teeth and was twisted down.

The last thing he saw was a deep elevator shaft that fell away for perhaps a mile into the earth.

He knew that it might take him two minutes to hit the bottom. He shrieked.

The worst thing was, he would be conscious . . . all the way down . . .

The rivers shook. The silver rivers trembled. The pathways, shocked, convulsed the metal shores through which they sped.

Wilder, traveling, was almost knocked flat by the concussion.

What had caused the concussion he could not see. Perhaps, far off, there was a cry, a murmur of dreadful sound, which swiftly faded.

Wilder moved. The silver track threaded on. But the City seemed poised, agape. The City seemed tensed. Its huge and various muscles were cramped, alert.

Feeling this, Wilder began to walk as well as be moved by the swift path.

"Thank God. There's the gate. The sooner I'm out of this place the happier I'll—"

The gate was indeed there, not a hundred yards away. But, on the instant, as if hearing his declaration, the river stopped. It shivered. Then it started to move back, taking him where he did not wish to go.

Incredulous, Wilder spun about and, in spinning, fell. He clutched at the rushing sidewalk.

His face, pressed to the vibrant grillwork of the river-rushing pavement, heard the machineries mesh and mill beneath, humming and agroan, forever sluicing, forever feverish for journeys and mindless excursions. Beneath the calm metal, embattlements of hornets stung and buzzed, lost bees bumbled and subsided. Collapsed, he saw the gate lost away behind. Burdened, he remembered at last the extra weight upon his back, the jet-power equipment that might give him wings.

He jammed his hand to the switch on his belt. And in the instant before the sidewalk might have pulsed him off among sheds and museum walls, he was airborne.

Flying, he hovered, then swam the air back to hang above a casual Parkhill gazing up, all covered with grease and smiling from a dirty face. Beyond Parkhill, at the gate, stood the frightened maid. Beyond even further, near the yacht at the landing, stood Aaronson, his back turned to the City, nervous to be moving on.

"Where are the others?" cried Wilder.

"Oh, they won't be back," said Parkhill, easily. "It figures, doesn't it? I mean, it's quite a place."

"Place!" said Wilder, hovered now up, now down, turning slowly, apprehensive. "We've got to get them out! It's not safe."

"It's safe if you like it. I like it," said Parkhill.

And all the while there was a gathering of earthquake in the ground and in the air, which Parkhill chose to ignore.

"You're leaving, of course," he said, as if nothing were wrong. "I knew you would. Why?"

"Why?" Wilder wheeled like a dragonfly before a trembling of storm wind. Buffeted up, buffeted down, he flung his words at Parkhill, who didn't bother to duck but smiled up and accepted. "Good God, Sam, the place is hell. The Martians had enough sense to get out. They saw they had overbuilt themselves. The damn City does everything, which is too much! Sam!"

And at that instant, they both looked round and up. For the sky was shelling over. Great lids were vising in the ceiling. Like an immense flower, the tops of buildings were petaling out to cover themselves. Windows were shutting down. Doors were slamming. A sound of fired cannons echoed through the streets.

The gate was thundering shut.

The twin jaws of the gate, shuddering ,were in motion.

Wilder cried out, spun round and dived.

He heard the maid below him. He saw her reach up. Then, swooping, he gathered her in. He kicked the air. The jet lifted them both.

Like a bullet to a target he rammed for the gate. But an instant before he reached it, burdened, the gates banged together. He was barely able to veer course and soar upward along the raw metal as the entire City shook with the roar of the steel.

Parkhill shouted below. And Wilder was flying up, up along the wall, looking this way and that.

Everywhere, the sky was closing in. The petals were coming down, coming down. There was only a last small patch of stone sky to his right. He blasted for that. And kicking, made it through, flying, as the final flange of steel clipped into place and the City was closed to itself.

He hung for a moment, suspended, and then flew with the woman down along the outer wall to the dock, where Aaronson stood by the yacht staring at the huge shut gates.

"Parkhill," whispered Wilder, looking at the City, the walls, the gates. "You fool. You damned fool."

"Fools, all of them," said Aaronson, and turned away. "Fools. Fools."

They waited a moment longer and listened to the City, humming, alive, kept to itself, its great mouth filled with a few bits of warmth, a few lost people somewhere hid away in there. The gates would stay shut now, forever. The City had what it needed to go on a long while.

Wilder looked back at the place, as the yacht took them back out of the mountain and away up the canal.

They passed the poet a mile farther on walking along the rim of the canal. He waved them off. "No. No, thanks. I feel like walking. It's a fine day. Good-bye. Go on."

The towns lay ahead. Small towns. Small enough to be run by men instead of the towns running them. He heard the brass music. He saw the neon lights at dusk. He made out the junk yards in the fresh night under the stars.

Beyond the towns stood the silver rockets, tall, waiting to be fired off and away toward the wilderness of stars.

"Real," whispered the rockets, "real stuff. Real travel. Real time. Real space. No gifts. Nothing free. Just a lot of good brute work."

The yacht touched into its home dock.

"Rockets, by God," he murmured. "Wait till I get my hands on you."

He ran off in the night, to do just that.

INDEX NOTE:

Ray Bradbury's fiction is often difficult to classify. Many of his stories are "borderline" cases: fantastic in mood and imagery, basically realistic in subject matter. "The Night" is just such a story — and is therefore *not* included in this listing. "The Invisible Boy" slips in, although its actual fantastic element is questionable. Parts of Ray's book, *Dandelion Wine,* contain near-fantasy; thematically, however, the book is nostalgic realism. I could go on — but the final choice on such stories was mine to make in this first-time attempt to isolate Bradbury's science fiction and fantasy from the bulk of his fiction.

Of his two hundred and fifty plus published stories, over one hundred and fifty are listed here. There are at least one hundred others which fall outside the science fiction or fantasy genre. As with Sturgeon and Oliver, none of his nonfiction is included, though, like Sturgeon, Bradbury has often dealt with science fiction in article and essay form. (Ray's total nonfiction output has recently topped the one hundred mark; his by-line has now appeared on more than four hundred separate items since 1940).

A Ray Bradbury
SCIENCE FICTION AND FANTASY INDEX

BOOKS:

Dark Carnival, Arkham House, 1947 (collection).

The Martian Chronicles, Doubleday, 1950 (collection). Contains interim bits and bridge passages written to unify the stories.

The Illustrated Man, Doubleday, 1951 (collection).

Timeless Stories for Today and Tomorrow, Bantam, 1952. Anthology, with Bradbury as editor.

The Golden Apples of the Sun, Doubleday, 1953 (collection).

Fahrenheit 451, Ballantine, 1953 (novel, with 2 ss).

The October Country, Ballantine, 1955 (reprints from *Dark Carnival*, plus 4 stories hitherto uncollected).

Switch on the Night, Pantheon, 1955 (juvenile).

The Circus of Dr. Lao and Other Improbable Stories, Bantam, 1956. Anthology, with Bradbury as editor.

A Medicine for Melancholy, Doubleday, 1959 (collection).

Something Wicked This Way Comes, Simon & Schuster, 1962 (novel).

R Is for Rocket, Doubleday, 1962 (reprints from earlier collections, with 3 stories hitherto uncollected).

The Machineries of Joy, Simon & Schuster, 1964 (collection).

The Vintage Bradbury, Vintage Books, 1965 (reprints from earlier collections, with 1 story hitherto uncollected).

S Is for Space, Doubleday, 1966 (reprints from earlier collections, with 4 stories hitherto uncollected).

IN MAGAZINES:
1941
"Pendulum" (with Henry Hasse), *Super Science Stories*, November.
1942
"Eat, Drink and Be Wary," *Astounding Science Fiction*, July.
"The Candle," *Weird Tales*, November.

1943

"The Piper," *Thrilling Wonder Stories*, February.

"The Wind," *Weird Tales*, March.

"Subterfuge," *Astonishing Stories*, April.

"The Crowd," *Weird Tales*, May.

"Gabriel's Horn" (with Henry Hasse), *Captain Future*, Spring.

"The Scythe," *Weird Tales*, July.

"Doodad," *Astounding Science Fiction*, September.

"And Watch the Fountains," *Astounding Science Fiction*, September.

"Promotion to Satellite," *Thrilling Wonder Stories*, Fall.

"The Ducker," *Weird Tales*, November.

"King of the Gray Spaces" (*R Is for Rocket*), *Famous Fantastic Mysteries*, December.

1944

"The Sea Shell," *Weird Tales*, January.

"Reunion," *Weird Tales*, March.

"The Monster Maker," *Planet Stories*, Spring.

"I, Rocket," *Amazing Stories*, May.

"The Lake," *Weird Tales*, May.

"There Was an Old Woman," *Weird Tales*, July.

"Morgue Ship," *Planet Stories*, Summer.

"Bang! You're Dead," *Weird Tales*, September.

"The Jar," *Weird Tales*, November.

"Undersea Guardians," *Amazing Stories*, December.

"Lazarus Come Forth," *Planet Stories*, Winter.

1945

"The Poems," *Weird Tales*, January.

"The Tombstone," *Weird Tales*, March.

"The Watchers," *Weird Tales*, May.

"The Dead Man," *Weird Tales*, July.

"Skeleton," *Weird Tales*, September.

"The Invisible Boy," *Mademoiselle*, November.

1946

"Final Victim" (with Henry Hasse), *Amazing Stories*, February.

"The Traveler," *Weird Tales*, March.

"Defense Mech," *Planet Stories*, Spring.

"Rocket Skin," *Thrilling Wonder Stories*, Spring.

"Her Eyes, Her Lips, Her Limbs" (as "William Elliott"), *Californian*, June.

"Chrysalis," *Amazing Stories*, July.

"Lorelei of the Red Mist" (with Leigh Brackett), *Planet Stories*, Summer.

"The Million Year Picnic," *Planet Stories*, Summer.

"The Homecoming," *Mademoiselle*, October.

"The Creatures That Time Forgot" ("Frost and Fire"), *Planet Stories*, Fall.

"Let's Play Poison," *Weird Tales*, November.

"The Small Assassin," *Dime Mystery*, November.

1947

"The Handler," *Weird Tales*, January.

"The Man Upstairs," *Harper's*, March.

"Tomorrow and Tomorrow," *Fantastic Adventures*, May.

"The Cistern," *Mademoiselle*, May.

"Rocket Summer," *Planet Stories*, Spring.

"Interim," *Weird Tales*, July.

"Wake for the Living" ("The Coffin"), *Dime Mystery*, September.

"Interim" ("Time Intervening"), *Epoch*, Fall.

"Zero Hour," *Planet Stories*, Fall.

"The Irritated People," *Thrilling Wonder Stories*, December.

"The Emissary," "Uncle Einar," "The Night Sets," originals for *Dark Carnival*, Arkham House.

1948

"The Shape of Things," *Thrilling Wonder Stories*, February.

"Powerhouse," *Charm*, March.

"The Black Ferris," *Weird Tales*, May.

"Jonah of the Jove Run," *Planet Stories*, Spring.

"And the Moon Be Still as Bright," *Thrilling Wonder Stories*, June.

"The Earth Men," *Thrilling Wonder Stories*, August.

"Pillar of Fire," *Planet Stories*, Summer.

"The Long Years" ("Dwellers in Silence"), *Maclean's* (Canada), September 15.

"Fever Dream," *Weird Tales*, September.

"Mars Is Heaven" ("The Third Expedition"), *Planet Stories*, Fall.

"Referent" (as "Brett Sterling"), *Thrilling Wonder Stories*, October.

"The Square Pegs," *Thrilling Wonder Stories*, October.

"The Women," *Famous Fantastic Mysteries*, October.

"The Visitor," *Startling Stories*, November.

"The Off Season," *Thrilling Wonder Stories*, December.

"The Spring Night" ("Summer Night"), *Arkham Sampler*, Winter.

"Asleep in Armageddon" ("Perchance to Dream"), *Planet Stories*, Winter.

1949

"The Silence," *Super Science Stories*, January.

"The Man," *Thrilling Wonder Stories*, February.

"The Silent Towns," *Charm*, March.

"Marionettes, Inc.," *Startling Stories*, March.

"The Concrete Mixer," *Thrilling Wonder Stories*, April.

"I, Mars," *Super Science Stories*, April,

"The Lonely Ones," *Startling Stories*, July.

"Changeling," *Super Science Stories,* July.

"The One Who Waits," *Arkham Sampler,* Summer.

"The Naming of Names," ("Dark They Were and Golden-Eyed"), *Thrilling Wonder Stories,* August.

"Holiday," *Arkham Sampler,* Autumn.

"The Mad Wizards of Mars" ("The Exiles"), *Maclean's* (Canada), September 15.

"Kaleidoscope," *Thrilling Wonder Stories,* October.

"Impossible" ("The Martian"), *Super Science Stories,* November.

"A Blade of Grass," *Thrilling Wonder Stories,* December.

1950

"I'll Not Look for Wine" ("Ylla"), *Maclean's* (Canada), January 1.

"Payment in Full," *Thrilling Wonder Stories,* February.

"Outcast of the Stars" ("The Rocket"), *Super Science Stories,* March.

"Punishment Without Crime," *Other Worlds,* March.

"Carnival of Madness," ("Usher II"), *Thrilling Wonder Stories,* April.

"There Will Come Soft Rains," *Collier's,* May 6.

"To the Future," ("Fox and the Forest"), *Collier's,* May 13.

"The Highway," (as "Leonard Spaulding"), *Copy,* Spring.

"Forever and the Earth," *Planet Stories,* Spring.

"The Illustrated Man," *Esquire,* July.

"Way in the Middle of the Air," *Other Worlds,* July.

"Purpose" ("The City"), *Startling Stories,* July.

"Death-By-Rain," ("The Long Rain"), *Planet Stories,* Summer.

"The World the Children Made" ("The Veldt"), *Saturday Evening Post,* September 23.

"Death Wish" ("The Blue Bottle"), *Planet Stories,* Fall.

"The Bonfire," *Torquasian Times,* Winter.

"The Green Morning," "Night Meeting," originals for *The Martian Chronicles,* Doubleday.

1951

"The Fireman," (early version of *Fahrenheit 451*), *Galaxy,* February.

"The Last Night of the World," *Esquire,* February.

"The Other Foot," *New Story,* March.

"In This Sign," ("The Fire Balloons"), *Imagination,* April.

"The Rocket Man," *Maclean's* (Canada), May.

"The Beast From 20,000 Fathoms" ("The Fog Horn"), *Saturday Evening Post,* June 23.

"The Pedestrian," *The Reporter,* August.

"A Little Journey," *Galaxy,* August.

"Embroidery," *Marvel Science Fiction,* November.

"No Particular Night or Morning," original for *The Illustrated Man,* Doubleday.

"Here There Be Tygers," original for *New Tales of Space and Time*, Holt.

1952

"The April Witch," *Saturday Evening Post*, April 5.

"The Wilderness," *Today*, April 6.

"A Piece of Wood," *Esquire*, June.

"A Sound of Thunder," *Collier's*, June 28.

"The Smile," *Fantastic*, Summer.

"The Tombling Day," *Shenandoah*, Autumn.

"The Gift," *Esquire*, December.

1953

"Hail and Farewell," *Today*, March 29.

"The Murderer," *Argosy* (England), June.

"And So Died Riabouchinska," *Saint Detective Magazine*, June–July.

"Time in Thy Flight," *Fantastic Universe*, June–July.

"The Millionth Murder" ("And the Rock Cried Out"), *Manhunt*, September.

"A Scent of Summer," ("Scent of Sarsaparilla"), *Argosy*, (England), October.

"The Playground," *Esquire*, October.

"The Golden Apples of the Sun," *Planet Stories*, November.

"The Flying Machine," original for *The Golden Apples of the Sun*, Doubleday.

1954

"All Summer in a Day," *Fantasy and Science Fiction*, March.

"The Watchful Poker Chip (of H. Matisse)," *Beyond*, March.

"It Came From Outer Space," *Vargo Statten Science Fiction* (England), May. (This version not written by Bradbury, but is based on his film treatment).

"The Strawberry Window," original for *Star SF No. 3*, Ballantine.

1955

"The Dragon," *Esquire*, August.

1956

"Icarus Montgolfier Wright," *Fantasy and Science Fiction*, May.

"Next Stop, the Stars," ("The End of the Beginning"), *Maclean's* (Canada), October 27.

1957

"Almost the End of the World," *The Reporter*, December 26.

1959

"The Shoreline at Sunset," *Fantasy and Science Fiction*, March.

1960

"Death and the Maiden," *Fantasy and Science Fiction*, March.

1962

"A Miracle of Rare Device," *Playboy*, January.

"Nightmare Carousel," *Mademoiselle*, January.

"Come Into My Cellar," *Galaxy*, October.

1963
"Bright Phoenix," *Fantasy and Science Fiction*, May.
"To the Chicago Abyss," *Fantasy and Science Fiction*, May.
"The Vacation," *Playboy*, December.
1965
"The Kilimanjaro Machine," *Life*, January 22.
1966
"The Best of Times," *McCall's*, January.
1967
"The Lost City of Mars," *Playboy*, January.

THEODORE STURGEON

"Listen, I'm out here in the woods, working on a *Star Trek.* I'm not in contact with anybody."

It was Sturgeon on the phone, calling from the wilds of New York to tell me, in civilized California, why he was not at home when I wanted to reach him.

Actually, he was wrong about not being in contact with anybody. Eighteen books and over one hundred and seventy-five stories make certain that he's always in contact with somebody, somewhere. He's in *National Review,* dissecting the latest science fiction, or he's in *Sports Illustrated,* speculating on futuristic baseball, or he's in *Playboy* and *The Realist* writing about kinky computers, or he's on TV with *Star Trek,* or he's adapting screenplays into novels for Pyramid and Gold Medal, or he's in a new anthology such as this. (He's been in dozens, including a revolutionary appearance in *The Best American Short Stories of 1960,* with an entry from *Fantasy and Science Fiction,* the superbly crafted, moving story of an astronaut's flight to Mars, "The Man Who Lost the Sea." Nearly everything he writes is anthologized.

He's never out of contact, hasn't been for thirty years. He even pops up in other people's books. (See "Kilgore Trout" in Kurt Vonnegut's *God Bless You, Mr. Rosewater.*)

To say that Ted Sturgeon is a full-time writer who's been selling professionally for three decades is certainly true enough, but he's also been involved in a staggering number of other pursuits. In fact, Ted could serve as a classic example of the writer who has "done everything."

In his half-century of living, Sturgeon has served as an accredited seaman on tankers (he holds five ratings in the merchant marine), has driven tractor-trucks cross-country, worked in an oil refinery, sold ladies' hosiery door-to-door, played guitar for a square-dance orchestra in the Poconos, managed a luxury resort hotel in the West Indies, operated bulldozers and power shovels in Puerto Rico, served as Assistant Chief Steward at an overseas U. S. Army air base, became copy editor for the advertising division of Reeves-Ely labs, and served two and a half years with Time, Inc., beginning at *Fortune* in circulation and moving up to head all ad promotion for *Time*'s four international divisions. (And, along the way, he has fathered several bright children during three marriages!)

Is that *all?* Of course not.

Ted Sturgeon has been a gymnastics instructor, an auto mechanic, a political ghost writer, short-order cook, electronics repairman, woodworker, garbage collector, a glass-factory employee, a literary agent in Manhattan and a circus roustabout in Canada.

"My great ambition as a boy was to be a 'flyer' for Barnum and Bailey," he says. "I earned an athletic scholarship and fourth place in the AAU East Coast Championship for horizontal bar. Then, in my mid-teens, I got rheumatic fever, and a heart enlargement. No Barnum and Bailey. Instead, I went to sea for three years."

Sturgeon's first story sale, to McClure's syndicate in 1937, was a short newspaper effort for which he received five dollars. This encouraged him to try more fiction, and he sold thirty-nine more shorts to McClure newspapers over the next two years, all of them "realistic."

"Then a friend showed me a copy of *Unknown*—which immediately decided me in favor of the fantastic. I began to write for John Campbell. My first really successful story was 'It,' a horror tale set in the woods of my childhood."

Readers of *Unknown* and *Astounding Science Fiction* found that a major new talent had exploded into print.

The "Sturgeon touch," compounded of an intense originality and a deeply humanistic approach, set Ted apart from his fellows. No one wrote quite like this— and Ray Bradbury admitted (in an Introduction to Ted's first collection), "I split every Sturgeon tale down the middle and fetched out its innards to see what made it function. At that time . . . I looked upon Sturgeon with a secret and gnawing jealousy."

Yet, despite his magazine acceptance, Ted discovered that pulp rates were not conducive to steady eating, and he began working his way around the globe, writing when and where he could, using his variegated mental and physical skills to advantage, often just one nimble step ahead of starvation. ("Ever make a vegetable stew out of six cents' worth of soup greens?") His stories got better; his style matured. There was no mistaking his intense dedication to "the music of words." As he declared, "Our language with all its faults, is one of the most completely expressive in history . . . the rich sources of English have brought to it shades of meaning . . . unparalleled in other tongues. I'd rather write than eat, which I've often demonstrated."

He was born Edward Hamilton Waldo in 1918 on Staten Island, New York, which he remembers as "a place of dark woods and mystery." His great-grandfather was Bishop of Quebec, his maternal uncle was Archbishop of the West Indies and his mother was a Canadian poetess. She later remarried a Scot named Sturgeon—and it was he who allowed the boy to be legally baptized as Theodore Sturgeon. ("I'd always wanted to be called Ted.")

Young Sturgeon fought against all formal schooling and proudly declares, "I managed to flunk every single subject I ever took at one time or another, without exception. But I *did* learn to smoke, swim, gamble and cuss."

From Nudism to Dianetics, Sturgeon has always been a student of life itself, immersed in its soul-dazzling variety; he has welcomed its rewards, accepted its injuries. ("No one can achieve the stature of a man unless he has been unjustly hurt.")

Ted has always helped others, has won intense love and loyalty as a result. And when James Blish stated that "all of Sturgeon's major work is about love," he was quite correct; this subject is and has been the main source of Ted's fiction, the well from which he draws his stories and his characters. Blish added, "Love, for Sturgeon, is far from a limited subject, for he has stretched the word to include nearly every imaginable form of human relationship." Ted is equally absorbed in human communication. "When a man and a woman go to bed together they are communicating," he says. "And when some guy pokes another guy in the nose, that *too* is communication. It's just that the message is different."

He is a searcher, seeking love, communication, emotion which can be put to paper, trapped within the skin of a story. "I write what I write to find a way home. 'Home,' in this sense, is what one wants . . . I write long stories and short ones and angry ones and funny ones, so that they can be homes for me."

One of Ted's close friends, writer-editor Judith Merril, describes him as a man of constant paradox. "Ted is full of self-contradictions," she says. "He is blind and perceptive, rational and illogical, pedantic and lyrical, self-centered and warmly outgiving. Snob and vulgarian, athlete and aesthete, mystic and mechanic, he is detached and merry, humble and arrogant, over-mannered and deeply courteous. He's a man of elegant naturalness, thoughtful simplicity . . . and above all, he has *style*."

Indeed he has. As man *and* author. That style is in rich evidence in the following novella. "One Foot and the Grave" is full of Sturgeon's particular magic, his humor, his poetic images, his elfin girls, his ability to shock and delight; it is a story of fantasy and fear, beauty and suspense. And it takes place in deep woods . . . the woods of "It," the woods of New York, the dark, surprising mystery-brimming woods of Ted Sturgeon's childhood.

ONE FOOT AND THE GRAVE
Theodore Sturgeon

I was out in Fulgey Wood trying to find out what had happened to my foot, and I all but walked on her. Claire, I mean. Not Luana. You wouldn't catch Luana rolled up in a nylon sleeping bag, a moonbeam bright on her face.

Her face gleamed up like a jewel sunk deep in a crystal spring. I stood looking at it, not moving, not even breathing, hoping that she would not wake. I'd found that horror of a skull ten minutes ago and I'd much rather she didn't see it.

She stirred. I stepped back and sideward into a bear-trap. The steel jaws were cushioned by my heavy boot; they sliced through from instep to heel, but did not quite meet. All the same, it was a noise in the soughing silences of the wood, and Claire's eyes opened. She studied the moon wonderingly for a moment because, I presume, her face was turned to it. Then she seemed to recall where she was. She sat up and glanced about. Her gaze swept over me twice as I stood there stiff and straight, trying to look like a beech. Or a birch. I must be of the wrong family. She saw me.

"Thad . . ." She sat up and knuckled her eyes. Claire has a deep voice, and meticulous. She peered. "It—*is* Thad?"

"Most of me. Hi."

"Hi." She moved her mouth, chewing, apparently, the end of sleepiness. She swallowed it and said, "You've been looking for me."

"For years," I said gallantly. That might have been true. At the moment, however, I was in pursuit of my foot, and possibly some peace and quiet. I hadn't counted on this at all.

"Well, Lochinvar, why don't you sweep me into your arms?"

"I've told you before. You're everything in the world I need, but you don't strike sparks. Go on back to bed."

She shook her hair, forward, out and down, and then breathtakingly back. She had masses of it. In the moonlight it was blue-gray, an obedient cloud. "You don't seem surprised to find me out here."

"I'm not. The last thing I said to you in town was to sit tight, stay where you were, and let me handle this. The fact that you are here therefore does not surprise me."

"You know," she said, putting one elbow on one knee, one chin in one palm, and twinkling, "you say 'therefore' prettier than anyone else I ever met. Why don't you come over here and talk to me? Are you standing in a bear-trap?"

She was wearing a one-piece sunsuit. It was backless and sideless and the summer flying suit, hanging on the bush at her head, plus the light nylon sleeping bag, were obviously everything in the world she had with her. About the bear-trap I said, "Well, yes."

She laughed gaily, and lay back. Her hair spread and spilled; she burrowed into it with the back of her head. She pulled the sleeping bag tight up around her throat and said, "All right, silly. Stand there if you want to. It's a big boudoir."

I said nothing. I tugged cautiously at the trap, moving just my leg. The boot all but parted; the moon gleamed on the steel jaws, now only an inch apart and closing slowly. I stopped pulling. I hoped she would go back to sleep. I hoped the trap wouldn't clank together when it finally went all the way through. I stood still. There was sweat on my mouth.

"You still there?"

"Yup," I said.

She sat up again. "Thad, this is stupid! *Do* something! Go away, or talk to me or something, but don't just *stand* there!"

"Why don't you just go on to sleep and let me worry about what I do? I'm not in your way. I won't touch you."

"That I don't doubt," she said acidly. "Go away." She thumped down, turned away, turned back and sat up, peering. "I just thought . . . maybe you *can't*. . . ." She flung out of the bag and stood up, slim in the moonlight. I could see her toenails gleam as she stepped on the fabric. Her right toenails, I mean. Her left foot wasn't a foot. It was a cloven hoof, hairy-fetlocked, sharp and heavy. She was as unselfconscious about it as she was of the casual coverage her sunsuit afforded her. She came to me, limping slightly.

"Go on back to—let me al—oh for Pete's sake, Claire, I'm perfectly—"

She breathed a wordless, sighing syllable, all horror and pity. "Thad," she cried, "Your—your *foot!*"

"I didn't want you to know."

"How could you just *stand* there with that—that—Oh!" She knelt, reached toward my trapped foot, recoiled before she touched it and stayed there looking up at me with her eyes bright in the silver light, silver tear-streaks on her face like lode-veinings. "What shall I *do?*"

I sighed. "Keep your fingers away from the trap." I leaned back and pulled. The macerated leather of my high-laced hunting boot held, gave, held—and then the jaws whanged together, close-meshed. I fell back against a birch-trunk, banging my head painfully. Claire, seeing almost the entire foot dangling under the arch of the trap's jaws, started a shriek, then jammed it back into her mouth with her whole hand. I grunted.

"Oh," she said, "you poor *darling!* Does it hurt?" she added inanely.

"No," I said, rubbing my skull. "It was just my head. . . ."

"But your foot! Your poor foot!"

I began unlacing what was left of the boot. "Don't

bother your pretty little head about it," I said. I pulled the boot-wings aside and slipped my leg out of boot and woolen stocking together. She looked, and sat down plump! before me, her jaw swinging slackly. "Shut it," I said conversationally. "You really looked beautiful a while back. Now you look silly."

She pointed to my hoof. It was larger than hers, and shaggier. "Oh, Thad! I didn't know . . . how long?"

"About three weeks. Damn it, Claire, I didn't want you to know."

"You should have told me. You should have told me the second it started."

"Why? You had enough on your mind. You'd already been through all the treatment that anyone could figure out, and I was in on all of it. So when it happened to me, I didn't see the sense in making a federal case out of it." I shrugged. "If Dr. Ponder can't cure this no one can. And he can't. Therefore—"

Through her shock, she giggled.

"Therefore," I continued, "there was nothing left for me to do but try to find out what had happened, by myself." I saw her lower lip push out before she dropped her face and hid it. "What's the matter?" I asked.

"I—kind of thought you were trying to help just me."

Claire can switch from giggles to tears, from shock to laughter to horror to fright, faster than anyone I ever met. It goes all the way down too. I said, "Don't kid yourself. I don't do things for people."

"Well," she said in a very small voice, "that's what I thought, for a while anyway."

"You better get back in that sleeping bag. You'll catch cold," I said.

She rose and crept obediently back to the sleeping bag. Once into it, she said, "Well, you'll care if I catch cold."

I went and hunkered down beside her. "Well sure. I might catch it."

"You wouldn't get that close!"

"Oh, I don't know. I read somewhere that a sneeze can travel thirty feet."

"I hate you."

"Because I sneaked out behind your back and got a fancy foot just like yours?"

"Oh, Thad! How can you joke about it?"

I sat back and lifted my hoof, regarding it thoughtfully. I had found it possible to spread the two halves and relax suddenly. They made a nice loud click. I did this a couple of times. "I'd rather joke about it. How frantic can you get?"

"Thad, Thad . . . It's my fault, it is, it is!"

"Uh-huh. That's what I get for playing footsie with you in roadhouses. You're contagious, that's what."

"You're no comfort."

"I don't comfort stupid people. This isn't your fault, and you're being stupid when you talk like that. Does yours itch?"

"Not any more."

"Mine does." I clicked my hoof some more. It felt good. "What gave you the idea of coming out here?

"Well," she said shyly, "after you said you'd track this thing down for me, but wouldn't say how, I thought it all out from the very beginning. This crazy trouble, whatever it is, started out here; I mean, it developed after I came out here that time. So I figured that this is where you'd be."

"But why come?"

"I didn't know what you'd get into here. I thought you might—might need me."

"Like a hole in the head," I said bluntly.

"And I thought you were doing it just for me. I didn't know you had a foot like that too." Her voice was very small.

"So now you know. And you're sorry you came. And first thing in the morning you'll hightail it straight back to town where you belong."

"Oh no! Not now. Not when I know we're in this together. I like being in something together with you, Thad."

I sighed. "Why does my luck run like this? If I got

all hog-wild and feverish about you, you'd turn around and get short of breath over some other joker. Everybody loves somebody—else."

"You're thinking about Luana," she said with accuracy. Luana was Dr. Ponder's typist. She had taut coral pneumatic lips, a cleft chin, and a tear-stained voice like that of an English horn in the lower register. She had other assets and I was quite taken with both of them.

"If I were as honest about my feelings as you are about yours," I said, "and as loud-mouthed, I'd only hurt your feelings. Let's talk about our feet."

"All right," she said submissively. "Thad. . . ."

"Mm?"

"What did you mean when you said you'd seen me be beautiful?"

"Oh, for Pete's sake! Skip it, will you? What has that to do with feet?"

"Well. . . . Nothing, I guess." She sounded so forlorn that, before I could check myself, I reached out and patted her shoulder. "I'm sorry, Claire. I shouldn't brutalize you, I guess. But it's better than stringing you along."

She held my hand for a moment against her cheek. "I s'pose it is," she said softly. "You're so good . . . so good, and—and so sensible."

"So tired. Give me back my hand. Now; let's put all this fantastic business together and see what comes out. You start. Right from the beginning, now; somewhere, somehow, there's got to be an answer to all this. I know we've been over it and over it, but maybe this time something will make sense. You start."

She lay back, put her hands behind her head, and looked at the moon. She had to turn her head for this, because the moon was sinking, and there were knife-edges of light among the cords of her throat. "I still say it was the night I met you. Oh, don't worry; I won't get off on that again . . . but it was. You were just a face among faces to me then. A nice face, but—anyway, it was the Medusa Club meeting, the night we got talking about magic."

"I'll never forget that night," I said. "What a collection of neurotics! Saving your presence, ma'am."

"That's the only purpose of the club—to find those things which frighten neurotics and stare them down, and to keep on doing it until somebody drops dead. Score to date: umpteen-odd dead boogie-men, no dead people. Hence the discussion of magic that night."

"That makes sense. And I remember Ponder's point that we are not as far removed from the days of the witches and wizards as we like to think. We knock on wood; we slip bits of wedding-cake under our pillows; we hook fingers with each other when we suddenly say the same thing together, and so on and on. And he said that perhaps this subconscious clinging to ritual was not because of a lingering childishness, but because the original magic forces were still in operation!"

"That was it," said Claire. "And a fine flurry of snorts he got for that!"

"Yup. Especially from you. I still don't understand why you got so steamed up."

"I *hate* that kind of talk!" she said vociferously. "But I hated it especially hearing it from Dr. Ponder. Ever since I've known him he's been so reasonable, so logical, so—well, so wonderful—"

I grinned. "I'm jealous."

"Are you, Thad? Are you really?" she said eagerly; then, "No. You're laughing at me, you heel . . . anyway, I couldn't stand hearing that kind of poppycock from him."

I put out my cloven hoof and snapped it in front of her nose. "What do you think now?"

"I don't know what to think . . ." she whispered, and then, with one of her startling switches of mood, continued in a normal voice, "so the next day I decided to track down some of the old superstitions for myself. Heaven knows this part of the country is full of them. The Indians left a lot, and then the Dutch and the French and the Spanish. There's something about these hills that breeds such things."

I laughed. "Sounds like Lovecraft."

"Sounds like Charles Fort, too!" she snapped. "Some

day you'll learn that you can't laugh at one and admire the other. Where was I?"

"In the woods."

"Oh. Well, the most persistent superstition in these parts is the old legend of the Camel's Grave. I came out here to find it."

I scrabbled up some of the soft earth to make a pit for my elbow and a hummock for my armpit. I lay on my side, propped up my head with my hand, and was comfortable. "Just run off that legend again, once over lightly."

She closed her eyes. "Somewhere in this no-good country—no one's ever been able to farm it, and there's too much jimson weed and nightshade for grazing—there's supposed to be a little hollow called Forbidden Valley. At the north end of it they say there's a grave with something funny about it. There's no headstone. Just a skull. Some say a man was buried there up to his neck and left to die."

"The Amazon Indians have a stunt like that. But they pick an anthill for the job. Cut off the feller's eyelids first. After that, the potato race, ducking for apples and ice cream is served in the main tent."

"A picnic," she agreed, shuddering. "But there was never anything like that among the local Indians here. Besides, we don't run to that kind of ant either. Anyway, this skull is chained, so the story goes, with a link through the edge of the eye-socket. It's supposed to be a magician buried there. Thing is, the legend is that he isn't dead. He'll live forever and be chained forever. Nothing can help him. But he doesn't know it. So if anyone wanders too close, he'll capture whoever it is and put 'em to work trying to dig him out. The old tales keep coming out—kids who had wandered out here and disappeared, the old woman who went out of her head after she got back to town, the half-witted boy who mumbled something about the skull that talked to him out of the ground. You know."

"Why do they call it the Camel's Grave?"

"I don't know. Some say the magician was an Egyptian who used to ride a camel around. Some say it comes from some Indian name. The nearest I can find in the library to 'Camel' is 'ko-mai' which means the green stick they used to spit meat over a fire. But that's Winnebago, and there were no Winnebagos around here."

"Wait. You mean there were Indian legends about this?"

"Oh, sure. I dug those out. There are all sorts of stories. Some of them are shocking—I mean in a nice way." She giggled. "But they all have one thing in common—the imprisoned magician, who, by the way, was old, old as the hills. He wasn't an Indian either. They made that quite clear. And always Camel, or 'Grave of the Camel.' Just to mix that up even more for you, I looked up 'camel' in the dictionary and found out that the word is derived from 'Djemal,' which is Arabic, or 'Gamal,' which is Hebrew."

"Fine," I said bitterly. "Much progress. So go on with your little trip out here."

"That first time? Oh, nothing happened. I brought some chow and stayed out here about four days at the full moon, which is supposed to be the time when the Forbidden Valley can be found. I didn't see a soul but old Goo-goo running his traps. No one pays attention to Goo-goo."

"Not even people who step into one of his bear-traps? You're lucky you didn't bed down in it."

"Oh, don't blame him, Thad! He's a sweet old man, really. He's deaf and dumb, you know. He keeps out of people's way as much as he can. Comes in with a few skins every now and then and lives off the land. He could tell us a thing or two about Forbidden Valley if he could talk. But he can't even write. They say he doesn't mind the haunted hills because no one ever found a way to tell him about them. What he doesn't know can't hurt him. As for the trap, he put it where he thought it might do him some good, among the birches where bears sometimes come to hunt for bugs under the bark. Practically no one ever comes out here. When they do, it's their lookout, not Goo-goo's."

"Hey." I straightened up. "How can you be so

casual about bunking out here with a wildcat or two
and an occasional bear wandering around? There are
copperheads too, to say nothing of a trapper who must
be lonesome, to put it mildly."

"Why I—" She paused, wonderingly. "I never
thought about it, I guess. Thad—nothing ever hurt me.
I mean it. No dog ever bit me, no cat ever scratched
me. I don't seem to be very tempting to mos-
quitos. Once when I was a little girl a bull gored a
hired man who was walking across a field with me.
The bull bellowed and jumped and capered all around
me, but he didn't touch me. I've never even been stung
by a bee."

"You don't say." I considered her thoughtfully. "I
begin to see why I asked you out for a beer the night
of the meeting."

"Why, Thad?"

"Now don't get ideas. I just pegged you as being—
different, that's all. Not better—different. You puzzled
me. I've been a lot of places, Claire. Tropics. At sea.
Construction jobs. I've met a lot of people, but no one
like you."

"That again," she snorted. "People are always telling
me that, one way or another. And what's it get me?
The very first time I fall for a big dead-pan stranger,
he doesn't know I'm alive. All large muscles and bad
taste."

"What do you mean bad taste?"

"Luana."

"Now look. I won't bandy her about. Stay off the
subject, see?"

Surprisingly, she laughed. "Temper—temper," she
cautioned. "My, you roar purty. But back to the subject at hand. I was out here four days and nights,
wandering around, trying to find the Forbidden Valley.
Once I thought I had it. It was about midnight. The
moon was bright, like tonight. I was near here somewhere. There was a little swag in the ground with a
high bluff at one end. I went up to it. I tripped over
something. I don't know what it was. I almost *never*
fall over things but I sure did that time. I fell right on

top of some little animal. I hope I didn't hurt it. I
don't know what it was. It wriggled out from under
me and whizzed away fast as a deer-fly. I never saw
anything move so fast; a blur and it was gone. It was
about as big as a chipmunk, but longer—oh, three
times as long. I got a vague impression of pointed ears
and the funniest broad, flat tail. It was like nothing
I've ever seen."

"I thought nothing happened in those four days."

"Well—that couldn't be important. Oh; I see what
you mean. *Anything* might be important. All right.
Now—what else?"

"Goo-goo."

"Oh. I saw him once. Twice. The first time he was
setting a whip-snare in a clearing in the woods. I
waved at him and smiled and he nodded and gurgled
the way he does and smiled back. The second time I
don't think he saw me. He was out in the open. Early
morning. He was tramping round and round in a circle
in the grass. Then he stopped and faced the sun. He
did something with his knife. Held it out, sort of, and
touched himself on the shoulders and chin with it. I
don't remember very clearly. It didn't last long. And
that's all."

"Hmp." I plucked some grass and skinned it with
my front teeth, to get the juice. "Then you came back
to town and your foot went haywire."

"Yes. It only took about six days to get the way it
is. It was awful at first. The toes gathered, and the
whole foot began to get pointed. It was longer at first.
I mean, my foot straightened out like a ballet dancer's,
and I couldn't get my heel down. Then the whole
thing thickened up and grew shorter, and the tip turned
black and hardened and—"

I interrupted, "I know, I know. Had one once myself. Now, how many people did you tell about it?"

"Oh, nobody. I mean, Dr. Ponder, of course, and
then you. Dr. Ponder was so—so—"

"Wonderful," I submitted.

"Shut up. So *understanding,* I mean."

"That's an odd word to use."

"Is it? Anyway, he said I had a—a—"

"Chitinous podomorphia."

"Yes. How did you know?"

"You told me, right after he told you. Only *I* remembered it. Mine began shortly afterward, and I remembered it again." I spit out my grass and selected another stem. "A brilliant diagnosis."

"Thad . . . you—sometimes you say things in a way I don't understand."

"Do I?" In the growing predawn darkness, I could feel her sharp swift gaze on me. I said, "Go on. He treated the foot?"

"He bound it. It was very clever. As the foot changed shape from day to day he changed the bandages, so that it never looked any worse than a slightly sprained ankle. He seemed to know all about the trouble. He predicted the course of the trouble as it developed, and told me that it would go just so far and stop, and he kept me from getting frightened, and explained why I should keep it a secret."

"What did he say?"

"He harked back to the meeting, and the things that had been said. Especially about the readiness of people to believe in so-called mystical events. He said there was enough residual superstition in town to make life miserable for a girl with a cloven hoof. Especially for me."

"Why you especially?"

"Didn't I ever tell you? I thought I had. . . . See, my mother and father . . . they were engaged. I mean, they were each engaged to someone else. Dad came from Scoville way. That's eight miles or more on the other side of these woods. He didn't know Mother at all. He took to coming out here at night. He didn't know why. He couldn't help it. And Mother—she was about eighteen at the time—Mother jumped up from the dinner table one night and ran. She just *ran* out here. It's a long way. Granddad tried to follow her, but she ran like a deer. When he finally came huffing and puffing into the wood—it was a white night like tonight —and stopped to get his breath back, he heard a man calling, 'Jessica! Jessica!' That was Mother's name. Granddad followed the sound. It was out here in the open somewhere. Granddad climbed a rise and looked down and saw this young man standing with his arms out, calling and calling, turning every which way as he called. Granddad was going to yell at him but then he saw Mother. She was going down the slope ahead of him, walking slowly—he used to say 'as if the meadow was a grand marble stair, and she in a gold dress, for all she was tattered with thorns.'

"The two of them stopped two yards apart and stood there staring at one another for longer than it took Granddad to get to them. He had to yell twice or three times before she even knew he was there. She kept her eyes on the young man's face and just said, 'Yes, Father.' And Granddad bellowed at her to come home. She stepped to the young man—that was my dad— and she put a hand on his arm and said, 'He'll come too.' Granddad said, 'The hell he will!' He wouldn't talk to my dad, he was so upset and angry. 'I don't even know his name!' and Mother said quietly, 'No more do I. You'd better ask him, Father.' And that was how it was."

I sat up and crossed my legs, entranced. "You mean that was the first time they saw each other?"

She nodded, though by now I could barely see her, for the moon was gone and only its cold loom stood in the sky over the western hills. "The very first time," she said. "And they were together every minute they could be after that. They were married right away."

"How?"

She shifted uncomfortably as I asked it, and said, "By a judge. It wasn't a church wedding. It was quicker. People talked. They still talk. They have lots of ideas about what went on out here, but what I'm telling you is the truth. Anyway, Granddad got used to the idea very soon, though he was against it at first. Even the talk didn't bother him; those two lived in a world of their own. Nothing touched them. Dad made wood-carvings—clock cases and newel-figurines and so on, and Mother was with him almost every minute.

Granddad used to say if you pinched the one, the other'd say 'Ouch.' He said nobody could stay mad in that house; he knew because he tried. So . . . it didn't matter what people said." She paused, and I just waited. Later, questions.

Presently she said sleepily, "And it *doesn't* matter. My mother and dad are like that now. They always will be. Nothing can change what you remember."

I waited again. This was a long time. Finally I asked, gently, "Where are they?"

"They died."

She slept. Somehow the moon had moved around to the east again. No: it wasn't the moon. It was a cloudless dawn, a dilution; light staining the hem of the sky. I sank back with my elbow in the hole I had dug and my armpit on the me-shaped hummock, and looked at the sleeping girl. I knew now what the single thing was that made her different. She was as changeable as bubble-colors; she felt, immediately and noticeably, all the emotions except one. And that was her difference. She was absolutely fearless.

That story . . . so simply told, and then, "They died." Cloven hooves.

"They died." People like that . . . for a time I was angrier at such a death than I was, even, at the ugly excrescence that was once a foot. Dr. Ponder seemed to know a lot about these things. "Chitinous podomorphia." Oh, fine. That meant "Change of a foot into chitin—hoof, horn, and fingernail material." I hadn't gone to Ponder. I couldn't really say why. Maybe Luana was the reason for that. Somehow I couldn't take the idea of Luana writing up my case history on her neat file-cards. And there was no other doctor in town. Here was Claire with the same trouble, and I'd been in on that from the word go. I just did for my foot what Ponder had done for Claire's, and hoped that Luana would never hear about it. What girl would give a tumble to a man with a cloven hoof?

The sun poked a flaming forehead over the wall of hills. By its light I studied Claire's relaxed face. She was not beautiful, by any means. She had a round, pleasant face. When she laughed, a transverse crease appeared under her nose; she was the only human being with that particular upper lip that I had ever liked. Her lashes were thick but not long, and now, with her eyes closed, half the beauty she had was cloaked, for she had the most brilliant eyes I had ever seen. Her jaw was round and small, slightly cleft. She missed being square and stocky by fractional proportions.

"I must be out of my mind," I muttered. Claire was a wonderful person . . . a wonderful person. Genuine, honest, full of high humor, and, for me, no fireworks.

But Luana, the beautiful secretary of Dr. Ponder, now, that was a different story. She had an odd, triangular face and a skin that seemed lit softly from underneath. Her cheeks were a brighter rose than the sides of her neck but you couldn't tell just where the gradations began. Her hair was the extremely dark but vivid red of black-iron in a forge just beginning to heat. Her hands were so delicate and smooth you'd think they'd break on a typewriter, and her canine teeth were a shade too long, so that her head looked like a flower with fangs. She had one expression—complete composure. Her unshakable poise made me grind my teeth; some way, somehow, I wanted it broken. I don't think she had brain-one and I didn't care; it wasn't her brains I was after. Her face floated before me on the flames of the fireworks she generated in me, and there wasn't a thing in the world I could do about it. When I was in town I'd date her, when I could. On the dates we didn't talk. She danced sedately and watched movies attentively and ate pineapple frappés with delicacy and thoroughness, and I'd just sit there and bask, and count the seconds until, after I walked her to her gate, she closed it between us and leaned across for a demure kiss. Her lips were cool, smooth, and taut. Pneumatic. Then I'd stride away snarling at myself. "You're a bumpkin," I'd say. "You're all feet and Adam's apple." I'd tell myself I had a hole in the head. I called myself forty kinds of a fool. "There's no future in it," I'd say. I'd tell myself, "You know that ten years from now, when the bloom is off, she'll look like something the cat dragged in, her and her teeth." And thinking about the teeth would make me visualize those lips again, and—so cool!

Often, those nights, I'd run into Claire, who just happened to be in Callow's Friendly Drug and Meat Market buying a whodunit, and we'd get a soda or something and talk. Those were the talks where everything came out. I never got so thick with anyone so fast. Talking to Claire is like talking to yourself. And she told me, somehow or other, about the foot, right from the first. She didn't tell anyone else. Except Dr. Ponder, of course. . . .

What a strange person she was! It was inconceivable that she should not have questioned Dr. Ponder more about her foot—yet she had not. His prognosis was that the condition would stop at her ankle, and may or may not be permanent, and, for her, that was that. In the same situation anyone else on earth would be scrambling around from specialist to specialist between trips to a wailing wall. Not Claire. She accepted it and was not afraid.

A patch of sun the size of a kitten crept up the edge of her sleeping bag and nestled in her hair. After a pause to warm and brighten itself, it thrust a golden pseudopod around the curve of her cheek and touched her eyelid. She stirred, smiled briefly at what must have been a most tender dream, and woke.

"Good morning."

She looked at me mistily, and smiled a different smile. "I fell asleep."

"You did. Come on—stir your stumps. I want to show you something that I've discovered."

She stretched and yawned. "I was talking to you and I fell asleep right in the middle of it. I'm sorry."

"I'm glad. You got your beauty sleep." Her face softened, so I added, "You need it."

"You're so sweet, Thad," she said. "Much sweeter than gall. 'Bout like vinegar, when you try hard." She slid out of the sleeping bag and idly scratched her

hairy ankle. "If I had to choose between this thing
with you, and my ordinary old foot without you, I think
I'd keep the hoof. How do you make that noise with it?"

I showed her. She tried it. All she could get was a
muffled pop, like fingers snapping with gloves on. She
laughed and said I was a genius, and rose and climbed
into her flying suit. She had half-length boots, padded
inside to support her hoof. Once they were on, no one
could have guessed. While she was about these small
chores, and others concerning folding and stowing
the sleeping bag and breaking out some C and K
rations, I rescued my amputated shoe from the bear-
trap and, by cutting and piecing the leather straps,
made a sort of stirrup that would hold it together
once it was on.

When that was done, Claire, looking shapeless and
tousled in the loose-fitting coverall, handed me one
of the sticky-rich candy bars from the rations. "Thad,"
she said with her mouth full, "you just *wouldn't* go to
see Dr. Ponder. Why not? Don't you trust him?"

"Sure I trust him," I said shortly. Why mention that
I was keeping away from him because of Luana?
"Come on," I said.

We crossed through a neck of the forest to the rolling scrub-meadow on the other side, and down and across
the first little valley.

"This is where I was last night. There's something
just over the next rise that I want you to see. Last
night I was afraid you'd see it."

"What's so different about today, then?"

"I found out last night you're not afraid of anything."

She did not answer. I looked back at her. She was
grinning. "You said something nice about me," she
half-sang.

"Not necessarily. Sometimes fearlessness is nothing
more than rank stupidity."

She swallowed that silently. As we climbed the rise
she asked, "Will you tell me about the time you saw
me be beautiful?"

"Later," I said.

Abruptly she clutched my arm. *"Look!"*

"Where? What?"

"There!" She pointed. "No—there—there, see?" She pointed rapidly to the ground, to a rock, to a spot in midair to our left. "See?"

"What is it, Claire? A deer-fly? or spots in the eyes?"

"Just watch," she said with exaggerated patience. "The little animal I fell on that time—remember? It's all around here, and moving so *fast!*"

There are certain optical illusions where a missing object becomes vividly clear as soon as you know what to look for. I focused my mind's eye on what she had described as a tapering, fan-tailed monstrosity with two front legs and a blue-black hide, and suddenly, fleetingly, there it was, crouching against the sheer side of the bluff. It blinked at me, and then disappeared, only to pop into sight for a fraction of a second right in front of us. We moved back with alacrity as if pulled by the same string.

"I want out!" I gasped. "That's the thing that gave you the fancy boot!"

Somehow we were twenty feet back and still backing. Claire laughed. "I thought that was your specialty."

"You pick the dog-gonnedest times . . . get back, Claire! Heaven knows what will happen to you if it gets to you again!"

She stood still, peering. The thing, whatever it was, appeared twice, once a little to the right, once—and this time, for a full two or three seconds—over against the side-hill. It balanced on two forelegs, its head thrust out, its wide fluked tail curled up over its back, and it blinked rapidly. Its eyes were the same color as its skin, but shiny. It disappeared. Claire said, "It can't hurt us. Dr. Ponder said the condition would be arrested where it is."

I snorted. "That's like saying you're immunized against being bumped by a truck because one ran over you once. Let's get out of here."

She laughed at me again. "Why, Thad! I've never seen you like this! You're pale as milk!"

"You have so seen me like this," I quavered. "The last time you called me sensible. Remember?"

The blue-black thing appeared again almost under my feet. I squeaked and jumped. Then it was by Claire, inches away. She bent toward it, hand outstretched, but it vanished.

"Thad, it seems terribly excited. I think it wants something."

"That I don't doubt," I said through clenched teeth. "Claire. Listen to me. Either you will hightail with me out of this imp-ridden corner of hell, or you and that monstrosity can stay here and watch me dwindle."

"Oh, *Thad!* stop blithering. The poor little thing is probably ten times as frightened as you are."

"Oh no it isn't," I said with authority. "It's alive, isn't it?"

She snorted and squatted down in the grass, her hands out and close together. Simultaneously with my warning cry, the creature appeared between her hands. Very slowly she moved them together. I stood petrified, babbling. "Claire, don't, please don't, just this once how do you know what that thing might do, Claire. . . . Okay—it's small, Claire. So is a *fer de lance*. So is a forty-five slug. Please, Claire—"

"*Will* you stop that infernal chattering!" she snapped. And just before her closing hands could touch the beast it was gone, to reappear six inches to the left.

She rose and stepped forward gently, stooping. The poised animal—if it was an animal—waited until she was a fraction of an inch away and again bounded out of visibility and in again, this time a yard away, where it waited, blinking violently.

"I think it wants us to follow it," said Claire. "Come on, Thad!"

It moved again, farther away, and bounced up and down.

"Oh, Claire," I said at last, "I give up. We're in this together and we've got to depend on each other. Maybe you're right after all."

Surprisingly, there were tears in her eyes as she said, "I feel as if you had been away a long time and just got back."

I thumped her shoulder, and we went on. We followed the strange creature up the slope to its crest, where the creature disappeared again, this time, apparently for good.

Claire had been right, we found a moment later. Distantly, sunlight flashed on the windshield of Ponder's parked convertible, which was parked where the wood road skirted the desolate flatland. Nearing the foothills where we stood were two plodding figures, and it was easy to spot Ponder, for no one else in the area had his stooped height and breadth. He was so perfectly in proportion that he made normal people look underdone. The other, I noticed with a gulp, was Luana, with her contained, erect posture, and the sunlight, after its cold journey through space, reveling in the heat of her hair.

We went to meet them. I looked once at Claire, catching her at the woman's trick of swift comparative appraisal of Luana's trim plaid skirt and snug windbreaker, and I smiled. Claire's coverall was not a company garment.

"Thad!" the doctor boomed. He had an organ voice; in conversation it always seemed to be throttled down, and his shout was a relaxation rather than an effort. "And Claire . . . we were worried."

"Why?" asked Claire. We reached them. I buzzed right on past the doctor—"Hi, Doc,"—and took both Luana's hands. "Lu."

She looked up at me and smiled. Those lips, so taut, so filled with what strange honey . . . when they smiled they grew still fuller. She said Hello, and I thought, what's language for? what's poetry for? when two small syllables can mean so much . . . I held her hands so hard and so long that it may have been embarrassing. It was for me, anyway, when Claire's voice broke into my ardent scansion of Luana's eyes with "Hey! Svengali! Got her hypnotized yet?"

I released Luana, who looked Claire's rumpled flying suit up and down. "Hello, Claire," she purred. "Hunting?"

"Just walking the dog," said Claire through her teeth.

I met the doctor's eyes and he grinned. "Good of you to take all this trouble over Claire's trouble," he said. "She just told me you knew about it. Does anyone else?"

I shook my head, but said, "Why all the mystery, Doctor?"

"I certainly don't have to tell you that this is not an ordinary medical matter."

Claire said, "Let's go on up to the Wood and sit down and talk. It's getting hot."

"I'll tote that if it's heavy," I offered, indicating Ponder's black bag.

"Oh no. Just a couple of things I brought with me, just in case."

He and Claire started back up toward the Wood. I put my hand on Luana's forearm and checked her.

"What is it, Thad?"

"I just want them to get a little way ahead. Luana, this is wonderful. What on earth made him come out here? And with you?"

"I don't know. He's a strange man, Thad. Sometimes I think he knows everything. Nothing surprises him." We began to walk. "We were working this morning—he was dictating some letters—and he all of a sudden stopped as if he was listening to something. Next thing I knew we were on our way."

"Does he really know what's the matter with Claire's foot?"

She looked at me. Her eyes were auburn and most disturbing. "I'm not supposed to talk about it."

"She told me. It turned into a cloven hoof. I've seen it."

"Oh. Then why ask?"

I hadn't expected this kind of resistance. "I mean, does he know *why* it happened?"

"Of course he does."

"Well, why?" I asked impatiently.

"Why not ask him?" She shrugged. "He's the doctor. I'm not."

"Sorry I asked," I said glumly. I was annoyed—I think at myself. I don't know why, subconsciously, I always expected this vision to melt into my arms, and was always sticking my neck out. But that's the way it is when you get fireworks.

We walked on in silence. Claire and the doctor had disappeared into the Wood when we entered the edge of it. We stopped for a moment to look about. There was, of course, no path, and the windless growth muffled and absorbed sounds, so it was difficult to know which way they had gone. I started in, but Luana held me back. "I don't think they're that way."

"I'll yell," I said, but she put a hand to her mouth. "Oh, *no!*"

"Why not, Lu?"

"I'm—I don't know. You shouldn't, in here." She looked about the silent halls of the forest. "Please, Thad. Go look for them. I'll wait. But don't shout, please."

Completely puzzled, I said, "Well, sure, honey. But I don't get it. Is something the matter?"

"No. Nothing." Her arched nostrils twitched. "Go look for them, Thad. I'll wait here, in case they come back for us."

"You're sure you'll be all right?"

"Go on. Go on," she said urgently. I suddenly thought that for certain reasons I might be behaving tactlessly. I must have blushed like a schoolgirl. "Well, sure. I'll be right back. I mean, I'll find 'em and call you." I flapped a good-bye self-consciously and blundered off through the woods. That girl really threw me for a loss.

I followed the level ground until I emerged from the Wood at the other side of its narrow neck—just what I should have done in the first place. Doctor Ponder and Claire were out in the open fifty yards away, apparently waiting for us. I went to them. "We lost you," I said. "Luana's waiting back there. She didn't want to thrash around in the woods hunting for you. Hold on and I'll get her."

Ponder's big head went up, and his eyes seemed to

focus on something I couldn't see for a moment. Then, "Don't bother," he said. "She's all right. I wanted to talk to you two anyway. Let's go in the shade and sit down."

"But—will she be all right?"

"She'll be all right," he grinned. He had good teeth. I shrugged. "Everybody seems to know what's right around here but me," I said petulantly. "All right." I led the way to a thicket at the edge of the wood and plumped down with my back against a tree. Claire and the doctor joined me, Ponder setting his bag carefully within his reach.

"Now for heaven's sake tell us," said Claire, who had kept an amused silence during my jitterings about Luana. She turned to me. "He wouldn't say a thing until you got here."

"Tell us about what? Who knows anything?" I said resignedly.

"You know about her foot," said Dr. Ponder. He looked down. "What, speaking of feet, has happened to your boot?"

I happened to be looking at Claire, and microscopically shook my head. "Oh," I said casually, "I left it on a railroad track while I was frog hunting in a culvert. Go on about Claire." Claire's eyes widened in astonishment at this continued deception, but she said nothing. I was pleased.

Ponder leaned back. He had a long head and a big jaw. The touch of gray at his temples and the stretched smoothness of his skin told lies about each other. He said, "First, I want to thank you both—you, Claire, because you have trusted me in this matter, when I had every reason to expect nothing but hysteria from you, and you, Thad, for having kept your own counsel. Now I'll tell you what I know. Please don't mind if I seem to wander a bit. I want you to get this straight in your minds." He closed his eyes for a moment, his brow furrowed. Then he wet his lips and continued.

"Imagine a man walking up to a door which stands firmly locked. He raises his hand and makes a certain motion. The door opens. He enters, picks up a wand.

He waves it; it suddenly glows with light. He says two words, and a fire appears in the fireplace. Now: could you duplicate that?"

"I've seen doors open for people in a railroad station," said Claire. "They had a beam of light in front of them. When you walked into it, a photoelectric cell made the door open."

"About that wand," I put in. "If it was made of glass, it could have been a fluorescent tube. If there was a radio frequency generator in the room, it could make a tube glow, even without wire connections."

"I once saw a gadget connected to a toy electric train," Claire said. "You say 'Go!' into a speaker and the train would go. You say 'Now back up' and it would back up. It worked by the number of syllables you spoke. One would make the train go forward; three would make it stop and back up. That fire you mentioned, that could be controlled by a gadget like that."

"Right. Quite right," said the doctor. "Now, suppose you fixed up all that gadgetry and took it back in time a couple of centuries. What would the performance look like to a person of the time—even an intelligent, reasonable one?"

I said, "Witchcraft." Claire said, "Why, magic."

Ponder nodded. "But they'd understand a kitchen match. But take a kitchen match back a couple more centuries, and you'd get burned at the stake. What I'm driving at is that given the equipment, you can get the results, whether those results can be understood by the observer or not. The only sane attitude to take about such things is to conclude that they are caused by some natural, logically explained agency—and that we haven't the knowledge to explain it any more than the most erudite scholar could have explained radar two centuries ago."

"I follow that," I said, and Claire nodded.

"However," said Ponder, "most people don't seem to accept such things that easily. Something happens that you can't understand, and either you refuse to believe it happened at all—even if you saw it with your own eyes—or you attribute it to supernatural forces, with all their associated claptrap of good and evil, rituals and exorcisms. What I'm putting to you is that everything that's happened to you is perfectly logical and believable in its own terms—but it's much larger than you think. I'm asking you to accept something much more mysterious than an r-f generator would be to a Puritan settler. You just have to take my word for it that it's as reasonable a thing as an r-f generator."

"I don't understand an r-f generator, as it is," smiled Claire. I heard the soft sound of her hoof clicking. "Go ahead, Doctor. At this point I'm ready to believe anything."

"Fine," applauded the doctor. "It's a pleasure to talk to you. Now, I'm going to use 'good' and 'evil' in this explanation because they're handy. Bear in mind that they are loose terms, partial ones: external evidences of forces that extend forward and back and to either side in time and space." He laughed. "Don't try to follow that. Just listen.

"A long time ago there were two opposed forces—call them intelligences. One was good and one was evil. It turned out to be quite a battle, and it went on for some time. There were gains and losses on each side, until one was captured by the other. Now, these intelligences were not living creatures in the ordinary sense, and in the ordinary sense they could not be killed. There are legends of such captures—the bound Prometheus, for example, and the monster under Yggdrasil. The only way to keep such forces imprisoned is to lock them up and set a watch over them. But, just as in our civilization, it may take profound intelligence and a great deal of hard work to capture a criminal, but far less intelligence and effort to keep him in jail.

"And that's the situation we have here. Not far from where we sit, one of those things is imprisoned, and he —I say 'he' for convenience—has his jailer.

"That's the thing known as 'The Camel's Grave.' The Camel is a living intelligence, captured and held here and, if right has its way, doomed to spend the rest of eternity here."

"That's a long time," I put in. "The earth won't last that long."

"He'll be moved in time," said Ponder complacently; and that was when I began to realize how big this thing was. There was that about Doctor Ponder which made it impossible to disbelieve him. I stared at Claire, who stared back. Finally she turned to him and asked in a small voice, "And—what about my foot?"

"That was a piece of tough luck," said Ponder. "You are a sort of—uh—innocent bystander. You see, the Camel is surrounded by . . . damnit, it's hard to find words that make sense! Fields. Look: if I call them 'spells,' will you understand that I'm not talking mumbo-jumbo? If I call them 'fields,' it presupposes coils and generators and circuits and so on. In this way 'spells' is more accurate."

"I'm with you so far," I said. Claire nodded.

"Well, the Camel is conscious. He wants out. Like any other prisoner, he looks through the bars from time to time and talks with his jailer—and with anyone else he can reach. What you stumbled into, though, wasn't the Camel: he's pretty well sealed away from that. You hit one of the spells—one of the small warning devices set there in case he should begin to escape. If it had hit him, it would have stung him a little, perhaps like an electric fence. But when you walked into it, you got that hoof. Why the result was exactly that I can't say. It's the nature of the thing. It's happened before, as mythology will tell you."

"I've thought of that," I said. "Pan and the satyrs, and so on. They all had cloven hooves. And isn't the Devil supposed to have one too?"

"One of the marks of the beast." Ponder nodded. "Now, as to what can be done about it, I'm here to do the best I can. Claire, exactly where was it that you walked into—whatever it was, and fell down on that little animal?"

"I don't know," she said calmly. "I haven't been able to locate it. I should be able to—ever since I was a child I've had dream compulsions to come out here, and I know this country like my own house."

"I wish you could find it. It would help." Ponder twiddled the catch on his black bag thoughtfully. "We have to try to get through to the Camel and let him know what has happened to you. He could counteract it. Well, anyway, we might be able to do something. We'll see."

"Doc," I said, "about that hoof. You're sure it was from contact with something out here. I mean, couldn't it have been something in town that caused it?"

"Positively not," he said. And I said to myself, now that is damned interesting, because I have a hoof too and I was never out here before last night.

Ponder turned to Claire. "Exactly why did you come out here that time you saw the little animal?"

"In a way it was your doing, Doctor. It was that Medusa Club meeting. You made me so mad with your intimations that there were still magical forces at work, and that superstitions served to guard humanity against them." She laughed diffidently. "I don't feel the same way now, so much. . . . Anyway, I know this part of the country well. I made up my mind to go to the most magical part of it at the most magical time—the full moon—and stick my neck out. Well, I did."

"Uh-huh," said the doctor. "And why did you come out yesterday?"

"To find Thad."

"Well, Thad? What were you after?"

"I wanted to see what it was Claire had walked into."

"Didn't trust my diagnosis?"

"Oh, it wasn't that. If I'd found anything at all, I probably would have told you about it. I was just curious about the cause and cure of cloven hooves."

"Well, I could have told you that you wouldn't find anything. Claire might, but you wouldn't."

"How so?"

"Hasn't it dawned on you yet that Claire is something special? In a sense she's a product of this very ground. Her parents—"

"I told him that story," said Claire.

"Oh. Well, that was the Camel at work. The only conceivable way for him to break out of his prison is through a human agency; for there is that in human nature that not even forces such as the one which imprisoned him can predict. They can be controlled, but not predicted. And if the Camel should ever be freed—"

"Well?" I asked, after a pause.

"I can't tell you. Not 'won't.' 'Can't.' It's big, though. Bigger than you can dream. But as I was saying, Claire's very presence on earth is his doing."

"My parents were murdered," said Claire.

I turned to her, shocked. She nodded soberly. "When I was six."

"I think you're right," said Ponder. "Their marriage was a thing that could cancel many of the—the devices that imprison the Camel. The very existence of a union like that threatened the—what we can call the prison walls. It had to be stopped."

"What happened?"

"They died," said Claire. "No one knew why. They were found sitting on a rock by the road. He had his arm around her and her head was on his shoulder and they were dead. I always felt that they were killed on purpose, but I never knew why."

"The Camel's fault," said Ponder, shrugging.

I asked. "But why didn't they—he—kill Claire too while he was about it?"

"She was no menace. The thing that was dangerous was the—the radiation from the union that her parents had. It was an unusual marriage."

"My God!" I cried. "You mean to say that Camel creature, whatever it is, can sit out here and push people's lives around like that?"

"That's small fry, Thad. What he could do if he were free is inconceivable."

I rubbed my head. "I dunno, Doc. This is getting to be too much. Can I ask some questions now?"

"Certainly."

"How come you know so much about all this?"

"I am a student of such things. I stumbled on this whole story in some old documents. As a matter of fact, I took the medical practice out here just so I could be near it. It's the biggest thing of its kind I've ever run across."

"Hm. Yet you don't know where the Camel's Grave is, exactly."

"Wrong," said the doctor. "I do. I wanted to know if Claire had been able to find it. If she had been able to, it would mean that the Camel had established some sort of contact with her. Since he hasn't, I'll have to do what I can."

"Oh. Anyone who can find the Grave is in contact with the Camel, then."

"That's right. It takes a special kind of person."

I very consciously did not meet Claire's gaze. There was something very fishy going on here, and I began to feel frightened. This thing that could shrivel a foot into a hoof, it could kill too. I asked, "What about this 'jailer' you mentioned. Sort of a low-grade variety of the Camel himself?"

"Something like that."

"That little animal—would that be it?"

A peculiar expression crossed the doctor's face, as if he had remembered something, dragged it out, glanced at it, found it satisfactory, and put it away again. "No," he said. "Did you ever hear of a familiar?"

"A familiar?" asked Claire. "Isn't that the sort of pet that a witch or a wizard has—black cats and so on?"

"Yes. Depending on the degree of 'wizard' we're dealing with, the familiar may be a real animal or something more—the concretion, perhaps, of a certain kind of thought-matrix. That little animal you described to me is undoubtedly the Camel's familiar."

"Then where's the jailer?" And as I asked, I snapped my fingers. "Goo-goo!"

"Not Goo-goo!" Claire cried. "Why, he's perfectly harmless. Besides—he isn't all there, Thad."

"He wouldn't have to be," said the doctor, and smiled. "It doesn't take much brains to be a turnkey."

"I'll be darned," I said. "Well, now, what have we got? A cloven hoof and an imprisoned *something* that must stay imprisoned or else. A couple of nice people murdered, and their pixilated daughter. All right, Doctor—how do you go about curing cloven hooves?"

"Locate the Camel's Grave," said Doctor Ponder. "and then make a rather simple incantation. Sound foolish?" He looked at both of us. "Well, it isn't. It's as simple and foolish as pressing a button—or pulling a trigger. The important thing is who does it to which control on what equipment. In this case Claire is the one indicated, because she's—what was it Thad said? —pixilated. That's it. Because of the nature of her parents' meeting, because of what they had together, because she is of such a character as to have been affected by the Camel to the extent of the thing that happened to her foot—it all adds up. She's the one to do it."

"Then anyone who's subject to this particular kind of falling arches could do it?" I asked innocently.

" 'Anyone'—yes. But that can't happen to just anyone."

I asked another question, quickly, to cover up what I was thinking. "About familiars," I said. "Don't I recall something about their feeding on blood?"

"Traditionally, yes. They do."

"Uh-huh. The blood of the witch, as I recall. Well how in time can the Camel character supply any blood to his familiar if he's been buried here for—how long is it?"

"Longer than you think . . . Well, in a case like that the familiar gets along on whatever blood it can find. It isn't as good, but it serves. Unless, of course, the familiar makes a side trip just for variety. Occasionally one does. That's where the vampire legends come from."

"How do you like that?" I breathed. "I'll bet a cookie that the animals Goo-goo traps are supplying blood to the Camel's familiar—and Goo-goo supposed to be guarding the jail!"

"It's very likely—and not very important. The familiar can do very little by itself," said the doctor. He turned to Claire. "Did you ever see anything like a familiar taking blood? Think, now."

Claire considered. "No. Should I have?"

"Not necessarily. You could though," he indicated her foot, "being what you are."

She shuddered slightly. "So I'm privileged. I'd as soon not, thank you."

I sprang to my feet. "I just thought . . . Luana. What could have happened to her?"

"Oh, she's all right. Sit down, Thad."

"No," I said. "I'd better go look for her."

Claire leaned back, caught her knee in her hands, and made a soft and surprisingly accurate replica of a wolf-howl. "Drop desperately ill," I said to her, and to Doctor Ponder, "That's for people you like too well to tell 'em to drop dead." And I strode off.

It took only a few minutes to regain the spot where I had left Luana. She was not there.

I stood still, my brain racing. Witches, wizards, familiars . . . people who could see familiars sucking blood, and people who could not . . . one more cloven hoof than the good doctor bargained for, and a theory that such a thing came from contact with Something out here, when I knew darned well I had acquired mine in town . . . a girl who did what her dreams told her to do and another with hair like hot metal and lips bursting with some cool sweetness. And where was she?

I moved into the Wood, walking quietly more because of caution for my torn boot than for any other reason, and peering into the mottled shadows. Once, with my eyes fixed on a distant clearing, I blundered into a nest of paper-wasps with my neck and shoulder. I started violently and moved back. The angry creatures swarmed out and around the damaged nest, and came after me as I sidled away, batting at them. They bumbled against my mouth and hair and forearms, but not one stung me. I remember thinking, when at last I was clear of them, that Claire had said something about bees . . . but before I could dredge up the thought I saw Luana.

If it had not been for the plaid skirt I couldn't possibly have seen her. She was as still as a tree-trunk in a little glade, her head bent, watching something which struggled on the ground. Moving closer, silently, I could see her face; and, seeing it, I checked any impulse I might have to call out to her. For her face was a mask, smooth, round-eyed, with curling lips and sharp white teeth, and it was completely motionless except for the irregular flickering of her nostrils, which quivered in a way reminiscent of a snake's swift, seeking tongue. Slowly she began to bend down. When I could no longer see her face I came closer.

Then I could see. I shall never forget it. That was when the fireworks went out . . . and a terrible truth took their place.

At the foot of a little bush was a bare spot, brushed clean now of loose leaves, doubtless by the struggles of the rabbit. It was a large brown-brindle rabbit caught in a whip-snare which had fouled in the bush. The snare had caught the animal around the barrel, just behind the forelegs, probably having been set in a runway. The rabbit was very much alive and frightened.

Luana knelt slowly and put out her hands. She picked the rabbit up. I said to myself, the darling! She's going to help it! . . . and I said, down deeper, but a woman looks tenderly at the thing she is about to help, and Luana's face, now, whatever it was, it wasn't tender.

She lifted the rabbit and bit into it as if it were an apple.

I don't know what I did. Not exactly. I remember a blur of trunks, and dim green. I think I heard Luana make a sound, a sigh, perhaps—even a low laugh. I don't know. And I must have run. Once I hit something with my shoulder. Anyway, when I reached Claire and the doctor I was panting hoarsely. They looked up at me as I stood panting, not speaking.

Then without a word, Ponder got up and ran back the way I had come.

"Thad! Oh, Thad—what is it?"

I sank down beside her and shook my head.

"Luana? Did something happen to Luana, Thad?"

"I'll tell you," I whispered. Something trickled down the outside of my nose. Sweat, I suppose. "I'll tell you, but not now."

She pushed my hair back. "All right, Thad," she said. And that was all, until I got my breath back.

She began to talk then, softly and in a matter-of-fact tone, so that I had to follow what she said; and the sharp crooked edges of horror blunted themselves on new thoughts. She said, "I'm beginning to understand it now, Thad. Some of it is hard to believe, and some of it I just don't *like* to believe. Doctor Ponder knows a lot, Thad, a whole lot. . . . Look." She reached into the doctor's bag, now open, and brought out a limp black book. On its cover, glittering boldly in a sunbeam, was a gilt cross. "You see, Thad? Good and evil . . . Doctor Ponder's using this. Could that be evil? And look. Here—read it yourself." She opened the book at a mark and gave it to me.

I wiped my eyes with my knuckles and took the book. It was the Bible, the New Testament, open to the sixth chapter of Matthew. The thirteenth verse was circled: It was the familiar formula of praise:

"Thine is the Kingdom, the Power, and the Glory, for ever and ever. Amen."

"Look at the bottom margin," she urged.

I looked at the neat block lettering penciled there.
"Ah-tay mahlkuth vé-G'boorah vé-Gédula lé o'lam, om," I read haltingly. "What on earth is that?"

"It's the Hebrew translation of the thirteenth verse. And—it's the trigger, the incantation Doctor Ponder told us about."

"Just that? That little bit?"

"Yes. And I'm supposed to go to the Camel's Grave and face the east and say it. Then the Camel will know that I have been affected and will fix the trouble. Doctor Ponder says that although he is evil—a 'black' magician—he can have no reason to leave me in this state." She leaned forward and lowered her voice. "Nor you either. You'll go with me and we'll both be cured."

"Claire—why haven't you told him I've got a hoof too?"

She looked frightened. "I—can't," she whispered. "I tried, and I can't. There's something that stops me."

I looked at the book, reading over the strange, musical sounds of the formula. They had a rhythm, a lilt. Claire said, "Doctor Ponder said I must recite that in a slow monotone, all the while thinking 'Camel, be buried forever, and never show yourself to mankind.' "

"Be buried forever? What about your foot? Aren't you supposed to say something about your foot?"

"Well, didn't I?"

"You did not." I leaned forward and looked close into her eyes. "Say it again."

" 'Camel, be buried forever, and never show yourself to mankind.' "

"Where's the part about the foot?"

She looked at me, puzzled. "Thad—didn't you hear me? I distinctly said that the Camel was to restore my foot and yours and then lie down and rest."

"Did you, now? Say it again, just once more, the way you're supposed to."

Obediently she said, " 'Camel, be buried forever, and never show yourself to mankind.' There. Was that clear enough? About the foot, and all?"

Suddenly I understood. She didn't know what she was saying! I patted her knee. "That was fine," I said. I stood up.

"Where are you going?"

"I have to think," I said. "Mind, Claire? I think better when I walk. Doctor Ponder'll be back soon. Wait here, will you?"

She called to me, but I went on into the Wood. Once out of her sight, I circled back and downgrade, emerging on the rim of what I now knew was the Forbidden Valley. From this point I could easily see the bluff at the far end. There was no sign of the skull. I began to walk down to where it should be. I knew now that it was there, whether it could be seen or not. I wished I could be sure of a few dozen other things. Inside, I was still deeply shaken by what I had seen Luana doing, and by what it meant—by what it made of me, of Claire, of Ponder. . . .

Behind me there was a horrible gargling sound. It was not a growl or a gurgle; it was exactly the hollow, fluid sound that emerges from bathrooms in the laryngitis season. I spun, stared.

Staring back at me was one of the most unprepossessing human beings I have ever seen. He had matted hair and a scraggly beard. His eyes were out of line horizontally, and in disagreement with each other as to what they wanted to look at. One ear was pointed and the other was a mere clump of serrated flesh.

I backed off a pace. "You're Goo-goo."

He gabbled at me, waving his arms. It was a disgusting sound. I said, "Don't try to stop me, Mister America. I know what I'm doing and I mean to do it. If you get too near me I'll butter these rocks with you."

He gargled and bubbled away like mad, but kept his distance. Warily I turned and went on down the slope. I thought I heard Claire calling. I strode on, my mind awhirl. Luana. Ponder. Claire. Goo-goo. The chained skull, and the blue-beast. The rabbit. Luana, Luana and those lips . . . *Ah-tay mahlkuth* . . . and a cloven hoof. I shook my head to clear my brain . . . *vé-G'boorah*. . . .

I was on level ground, approaching the bluff. "Get up, Camel!" I barked hoarsely. "Here I come, ready or not!"

Shocking, the skull, the famous mark of the Camel's Grave, appeared on the ground. It was a worn, weatherbeaten skull, worn far past the brilliant bleaching of bones merely desiccated and clean. It was yellowed, paper-brittle. The eyebrow ridges were not very prominent, and the lower jaw, what I could see of it, was long, firm. Its most shocking feature was part of it, but not naturally part of it. It was a chain of some black metal, its lower link disappearing into the ground, its upper one entering the eye socket and coming out through the temple. The chain had a hand-wrought appearance, and although it was probably as thick as the day it was made, unrusted and strong, I knew instinctively that it was old, old. It seemed to be—it *must* be—watching me through its empty sockets. I thought I heard the chain clink once. The bleached horror seemed to be waiting.

There was a small scuffling sound right at my heels. It was Goo-goo. I wheeled, snarling at him. He retreated, mouthing. I ground out, "Keep out of my reach, rosebud, or I'll flatten you!" and moved around to the left of the skull where I could face the east.

"Ah-tay mahlkuth vé—" I began; and something ran across my foot. It was the blue beast, the familiar. It balanced by the skull, blinking, and disappeared. I looked up to see Goo-goo approaching again. His face was working; he was babbling and drooling.

"Keep clear," I warned him.

He stopped. His clawlike hand went to his belt. He drew a horn-handled sheath knife. It was blue and keen. I had some difficulty in separating my tongue from the roof of my mouth. I stood stiffly, trying to brace myself the way an alerted cat does, ready to leap in any direction, or up, or flat down.

Goo-goo watched me. He was terrifying because he did not seem particularly tense, and I did not know what he was going to do. What was he, anyway? Surely more than a crazy deaf-mute, mad with loneliness. Was he really the jailer of a great Power? Or was he, in some way, in league with that disappearing bad-dream of a familiar?

I began again: *"Ah-tay mahlkuth vé-G'boor—"* and again was distracted by the madman. For instead of threatening me with his glittering blade, he was performing some strange manual of arms with it, moving it from shoulder to shoulder as I spoke, extending it outward, upward . . . and he stopped when I stopped, looking at me anxiously.

At last there seemed to be some pattern, some purpose, to what he was trying to do. When I spoke a certain phrase, he made a certain motion with the knife. *"Ah-tay . . ."* I said experimentally. He touched his forehead with the knife. I tried it again; he did it again. Slowly, then, without chanting, I recited the whole rigmarole. Following me attentively, he touched his forehead, his chest, his right shoulder, his left, and on the final *"om"* he clasped his hands together with the point of the knife upward.

"Okay, chum," I said. "Now what?"

He immediately extended the knife to me, hilt first. Amazed, I took it. He nodded encouragingly and babbled. He also smiled, though the same grimace a few minutes earlier, before I was convinced of his honest intentions, would have looked like a yellow-fanged snarl to me. And upon me descended the weight of my appalling ignorance. How much difference did the knife make to the ritual? Was it the difference between blanks and slugs in a gun? Or was it the difference between pointing it at myself or up in the air?

Ponder would know. Ponder, it developed, did, and he told me, and I think he did it in spite of himself. As I stood there staring from the steel to the gibbering Goo-goo, Ponder's great voice rolled down to me from the Wood end of the vale. *"Thad! Not with the knife!"*

I glanced up. Ponder was coming down as fast as he could, helping Claire with one hand and all but dragging Luana with the other. Goo-goo began to dance with impatience, guggling away like an excited ape, pointing at me, at his mouth, at the knife, the staring skull. The blue beast flickered into sight between his legs, beside him, on his shoulder, and for a brief moment on his head, teetering there like some surrealistic plume. I took all this in and felt nothing but utter confusion.

Claire called, "Put down the knife, Thad!"

Something—some strange impulse from deep inside me, made me turn and grin at them as they scurried down toward me. I bellowed, "Why, Doc! I don't qualify, do I?"

Ponder's face purpled. "Come out of there!" he roared. "Let Claire do it!"

I reached down and yanked the makeshift stirrup from my boot, laughing like a maniac. I kicked off the toe of the boot with its padding, and hauled the rest up my leg. "What's she got that I haven't got?" I yelled.

Ponder, still urging the girls forward, turned on Luana. "You see? He saw you feeding! He could *see* you! You should have known!" and he released her and backhanded her viciously. She rolled with the blow deftly, but a lot of it connected. It was not she, however, but Claire who gasped. Luana's face was as impassive as ever. I grunted and turned to face the skull, raising the knife. "How's it go, little man?" I asked Goo-goo. I put the point of the knife on my forehead. "That it?"

He nodded vociferously, and I began to chant.

"*Ah-tay . . .*" I shifted the knife downward to my chest. Ponder was bellowing something. Claire screamed my name.

"*Mahlkuth. . . .*" With part of my mind I heard, now, what Ponder was yelling. "You'll free him! Stop it, you fool, you'll free him!" And Claire's voice again: "A gun. . . ." I thought, down deep inside, *Free him!* I put the knife-point on my right shoulder.

"*Vé-G'boorah!*" There was the sharp bark of a shot. Something hit the small of my back. The blue beast stumbled from between my feet, and as I shifted the knife to my left shoulder, I saw it bow down and, with its mouth, lay something at my feet. It teetered there for a split second, its eyes winking like fan-blades in bright light, and I'll swear the little devil grinned at me. Then it was gone, leaving behind a bullet on the grass.

"*Vé-Gédula . . .*" I chanted, conscious that so far I had not broken the compelling rhythm of the ancient syllables, nor missed a motion with the knife. Twice more the gun yapped, and with each explosion I was struck, once in the face, once on the neck. Not by bullets, however, but by the cold rubbery hide of the swift familiar, which dropped in front of me with its

little cheeks bulging out like those of a chipmunk at
acorn time. It put the two bullets down by the first
and vanished. I clasped my hands on the knife-hilt,
pressing it to my chest, point upward the way Goo-
goo had done.

"Lé o'lam. . . ." From the corner of my eye I saw
Ponder hurling himself at me, and the ragged figure
of little Goo-goo rising up between us. Ponder struck
the little man aside with one bear-like clubbing of his
forearm, and was suddenly assaulted either by fifty
of the blue familiars or by one moving fifty times as
fast as a living thing ought to. It was in his ears, flutter-
ing on his face, nipping the back of his neck, clawing
at his nostrils, all at once. Ponder lost one precious
second in trying to bat the thing away, and then apparently decided to ignore it. He launched himself at
me with a roar, just as I came out with the final syllable of the incantation: *"OM!"*

It isn't easy to tell what happened then. They say
The Egg hit Hiroshima with "a soundless flash." It
was like that. I stood where I was, my head turned
away from the place where the skull had been, my
eyes all but closed against that terrible cold radiance.
Filtering my vision through my lashes, I saw Ponder
still in midair, still coming toward me. But as he
moved, he—changed. For a second he must have been
hot, for his clothes charred. But he was cold when he
hit me, cold as death. His clothes were a flurry of
chilled soot; his skin was brittle, frigid eggshell through
which his bones burst and powdered. I stood, braced
for a solid impact that never came, showered with the
scorched and frozen detritus of what had been a man.

Still I stood, holding the knife, for hardly a full
second had passed; and my vision went out with that
blinding light. I saw Claire thirty yards away on her
knees, her face in her hands; and whether she had
fallen or was praying I could not know. Goo-goo was
on the ground where Ponder had stretched him, and
near his body was the familiar, still at last. Beyond
stood Luana, still on her feet, her auburn eyes blindly
open to the great light, her face composed. She stepped

forward slowly, hanging her arms, but with her head erect, her heated hair flung back. The cruel, steady light made sharp-edged shadows on the hinges of her jaw, for all they were sunlit. For a brief moment she was beautiful, and then she seemed to be walking down a staircase, for she grew shorter as she walked. Her taut skin billowed suddenly like a pillow-slip on a clothesline, and her hair slipped down and drifted off in a writhing cloud. She opened her mouth, and it made a triangle, and she began to bleat.

They were wordless sounds, each one higher in pitch than the one before. Up and up they went, growing fainter as they grew higher, turning to rat-squeaks, mouse-squeaks, bat-squeaks, and at last a high thin whistle that was not a sound at all but a pressure on the eardrums. Suddenly there was nothing moving there at all; there was only a plaid skirt and a windbreaker tumbled together with blood on them. And a naked, lizard-like thing nosed out of the pathetic pile, raised itself up on skinny forelimbs, sniffed with its pointed snout at the light, and fell dead.

Claire drew a long, gasping breath. The sound said nothing for Claire, but much for the vale. It said how utterly quiet it was. I looked again at the plaid skirt lying tumbled on the grass, and I felt a deep pain. I did not mourn Luana, for Luana never was a woman; and I knew now that had I never seen her again after our last kiss over the gate, I would not have remembered her as a woman. But she had been beauty; she had been cool lips and infernal hair, and skin of many subtle sorts of rose; I mourned these things, in the face of which her lack of humanity was completely unimportant.

The light dimmed. I dropped the knife and went to Claire. I sank down beside her and put my arms around her. She let her hands slide off her face and turned it into my shoulder. She was not crying. I patted her hair, and we rested there until I was moved to say, "We can look at him now," and for a moment longer while we enjoyed the awe of knowing that all the while he had been standing there, released.

Then, together, we turned our heads and looked at him.

He had dimmed his pent-up light, but still he blazed. I will not say what he looked like, because he looked like only himself. I will not say he looked like a man, because no man could look like him. He said, "Claire, take off your boot."

She bent to do it, and when she had, something flowed from him to us. I had my hoof under me. I felt it writhe and swell. There was an instant of pain. I grasped the hairy ankle as the coarse hair fell out, and then my foot was whole again. Claire laughed, patting and stroking her restored foot. I had never seen her face like that before.

Then *he* laughed. I will not say what that was like either. "Thad, Thad, you've done it. You've bungled and stumbled, but you've done it." I'll say how he spoke, though. He spoke like a man.

"What have I done?" I asked. "I have been pushed and pulled; I've thought some things out, and I've been both right and wrong—what have I done?"

"You have done right—finally," he chuckled. "You have set me free. You have broken walls and melted bars that are inconceivable to you . . . I'll tell you as much as I can, though.

"You see, for some hundreds of thousands of years I have had a—call it a jailer. He did not capture me: that was done by a far greater one than he. But the jailer's name was Korm. And sometimes he lived as a bird and sometimes as an animal or a man. You knew him as Ponder. He was a minor wizard, and Luana was his familiar. I too have a familiar—Tiltol there." He indicated the blue beast, stretched quietly out at his feet.

"Imprisoned, I could do very little. Korm used to amuse himself by watching my struggles, and occasionally he would set up a spell to block me even further. Sometimes he would leave me alone, to get my hopes up, to let me begin to free myself, so that he could step in and check me again, and laugh. . . .

"One thing I managed to do during one of those

periods was to bring Claire's parents together. Korm thought that the magic thing they had between them was the tool I was developing, and when it began to look like a strong magic, he killed them. He did not know until much later that Claire was my magic; and when he found it out, he made a new and irritating spell around me, and induced Claire to come out here and walk into it. It was supposed to kill her, but she was protected; all it did was to touch her with the mark of the beast—a cloven hoof. And it immobilized me completely for some hours.

"When I could, I sent Tiltol after her with a new protection; without it she would be in real danger from Korm, for he was bound to find out how very special she was. Tiltol tried to weave the new protection around her—and found that he could not. Her aura was no longer completely her own. She had fallen in love; she had given part of herself away to you, Thad. Now, since the new spell would work only on one in Claire's particular condition, and since he could not change that, Tiltol found a very logical solution: He gave you a cloven hoof too, and then cast the protection over both of you. That's why the bear-trap did not hurt you, and why the wasps couldn't sting you."

"I'm beginning to see," I said. "But—what's this about the ritual? How did it set you free?"

"I can't explain that. Roughly, though, I might say that if you regard my prison as locked, and your presence as the key in the lock, then the ritual was the turning of the key, and the use of the knife was the direction in which the key was turned. If you— or Claire, which was Korm's intention—had used the ritual without the knife, I would have been more firmly imprisoned than ever, and you two would have lived out your lives with those hooves."

"What about Goo-goo? I thought for a while that he was the jailer."

He chuckled. "Bless you, no. He is what he seems to be—a harmless, half-demented old man, keeping himself out of people's way. He isn't dead, by the way. When he wakes, he'll have no recollection of all this. I practiced on him, to see if I could get a human being to perform the ritual, and he has been a good friend. He won't lose by it. Speaking of the ritual, though, I'd like you to know that, spectacular as it might have been, it wasn't the biggest part of the battle. That happened before—when you and Claire were talking to Ponder. Remember when Claire recited the spell and didn't know what she was saying?"

"I certainly do. That was when I suddenly decided there was something funny about Ponder's story. He had hypnotized her, hadn't he?"

"Something very like it . . . he was in her mind and I, by the way, was in yours. That's what made you leap up and go to Luana."

I shuddered. "That was bad . . . evil. What about this 'good and evil' theory of Ponder's, incidentally? How could he have worked evil on you with a spell from the Bible?"

There was a trace of irritation in his voice. "You'll have to get rid of this 'black and white magic' misconception," he said. "Is a force like electricity 'white' or 'black'? You use it for the iron lung. You use it also for the electric chair. You can't define magic by its methods and its materials, but only in terms of its purpose. Regard it, not as 'black' and 'white' but as High and Low magic. As to the Testament, why, that ritual is older than the Bible or it couldn't have been recorded there. Believe me, Ponder was using it well out of its context. Ah well, it's all over with now. You two are blessed—do you realize that? You both will keep your special immunity, and Claire shall have what she most wants, besides."

"What about you?"

"I must go. I have work to do. The world was not ordained to be without me.

"For there is reason in the world, and all the world is free to use it. But there has been no will to use it. There's wilfulness aplenty, in individuals and in groups, but no great encompassing will to work with reason. Almost no one reads a Communist newspaper but Communists, and only prohibitionists attend a dry convention. Humanity is split up into tiny groups, each clinging to some single segment of Truth, and earnestly keeping itself unaware of the other Truths that make up the great mosaic. And even when humans are aware of the fact that others share the same truth, they allow themselves to be kept apart from each other. The farmer here knows that the farmer there does not want to fight a war against him, yet they fight. I am that Will. I am the brother of Reason, who came here with me. My brother has done well, but he needs me, and you have set me free."

"Who are you?" I asked.

"The earliest men called me Kamäel."

"The Camel . . . in every language," murmured Claire. Suddenly her eyes widened. "You are—an . . . an *archangel,* Kamäel! I've read . . ."

He smiled, and we looked down, blinded.

"Tiltol!"

The tiny familiar twitched and was suddenly balancing on its two legs. It moved abruptly, impossibly fast, zoomed up to Kamäel, where it nestled in the crook of his arm. And suddenly it began to grow and change. Great golden feathers sprouted from its naked hide, and a noble crest. It spread wide wings. Its plumage was an incredible purple under its golden crest and gold-tipped wings. We stared, filling our minds with a sight no human being alive had seen—of all birds, the noblest.

"Good-bye," said Kamäel. "Perhaps one day you will know the size of the thing you have done. The One who imprisoned me will come back, one day, and we will be ready for him."

"Satan?"

"Some call him that."

"Did he leave earth?"

"Bless you, yes! Mankind has had no devil but himself these last twenty thousand years! But we'll be ready for the Old One, now."

There was more sun, there were more colors in the world as we walked back to town.

"It was the Phoenix!" breathed Claire for the twentieth time. "What a thing to tell our children."

"Whose children?"

"Ours."

"Now look," I said, but she interrupted me. "Didn't he say I was to have what I wanted most?"

I looked down at her, trying hard not to smile. "Oh, all right," I said.

A Theodore Sturgeon
SCIENCE FICTION AND FANTASY INDEX

BOOKS:
Without Sorcery, Prime Press, 1948 (collection).
The Dreaming Jewels, Greenberg, 1950 (novel).
E Pluribus Unicorn, Abelard Press, 1953 (collection).
More Than Human, Farrar, Straus & Young and Ballantine Books, 1953 (novel, formed as three unified novelettes).
A Way Home, Funk & Wagnalls, 1955 (collection).
Caviar, Ballantine Books, 1955 (collection).
A Touch of Strange, Doubleday, 1958 (collection).
The Cosmic Rape, Dell, 1958 (novel).
Aliens 4, Avon, 1959 (collection).
Beyond, Avon, 1960 (collection).
Venus Plus x, Pyramid, 1960 (novel).
Voyage to the Bottom of the Sea, Pyramid, 1961 (adapted novel).
Sturgeon in Orbit, Pyramid, 1964 (collection).
Starshine, Pyramid, 1966 (collection, reprints from earlier collections, with 3 hitherto uncollected stories).

IN MAGAZINES:
1939
"Ether Breather," *Astounding Science Fiction*, September.
"A God in a Garden," *Unknown*, October.
1940
"Derm Fool," *Unknown*, March.
"He Shuttles," *Unknown*, April.
"It," *Unknown*, August.
"Butyl and the Breather," *Astounding Science Fiction*, October.
"Cargo," *Unknown*, November.
1941
"Completely Automatic," *Astounding Science Fiction*, February.

"The Ultimate Egoist," (as "E. Hunter Waldo,"), *Unknown*, February.

"Shottle Bop," *Unknown*, February.

"Poker Face," *Astounding Science Fiction*, March.

"Microcosmic God," *Astounding Science Fiction*, April.

"The Haunt," *Unknown*, April.

"Nightmare Island" (as "E. Waldo Hunter"), *Unknown*, June.

"Yesterday Was Monday," *Unknown*, June.

"Artnan Process," *Astounding Science Fiction*, June.

"The Purple Light" (as "E. Waldo Hunter"), *Astounding Science Fiction*, June.

"Biddiver," *Astounding Science Fiction*, August.

"The Golden Egg," *Unknown*, August.

"Two Percent Inspiration," *Astounding Science Fiction*, October.

"Brat," *Unknown*, December.

1942

"Medusa," *Astounding Science Fiction*, February.

"The Jumper," *Unknown*, August.

"The Hag Saleen" (with James H. Beard), *Unknown*, December.

1943

"The Green-Eyed Monster," *Unknown*, June.

"The Bones" (with James H. Beard), *Unknown*, August.

1944

"Killdozer," *Astounding Science Fiction*, November.

1946

"Memorial," *Astounding Science Fiction*, April.

"The Chromium Helmet," *Astounding Science Fiction*, June.

"Mewhu's Jet," *Astounding Science Fiction*, November.

1947

"Cellmate," *Weird Tales*, January.

"Blabbermouth," *Amazing*, February.

"Maturity," *Astounding Science Fiction*, February.

"Fluffy," *Weird Tales*, March.

"Tiny and the Monster," *Astounding Science Fiction*, May.

"Bianca's Hands," *Argosy* (England), May.

"The Sky Was Full of Ships," *Thrilling Wonder Stories*, June.

"Largo," *Fantastic Adventures*, July.

"Unite and Conquer," *Astounding Science Fiction*, October.

"Thunder and Roses," *Astounding Science Fiction*, November.

1948

"Deadly Ratio," *Weird Tales*, January.

"There is No Defense," *Astounding Science Fiction*, February.

"The Professor's Teddy Bear," *Weird Tales*, March.

"Abreaction," *Weird Tales*, July.

"Memory," *Thrilling Wonder Stories*, August.

"That Low," *Famous Fantastic Mysteries*, October.

"The Perfect Host," *Weird Tales*, November.

"The Love of Heaven," *Astounding Science Fiction*, November.
"The Graveyard Reader," original for anthology of same title, Ballantine.

1949

"Messenger," *Thrilling Wonder Stories*, February.
"The Martian and the Moron," *Weird Tales*, March.
"Prodigy," *Astounding Science Fiction*, April.
"Minority Report," *Astounding Science Fiction*, June.
"One Foot and the Grave," *Weird Tales*, September.
"The Hurkle Is a Happy Beast," *Fantasy and Science Fiction*, Fall.
"What Dead Men Tell," *Astounding Science Fiction*, November.
"Farewell to Eden," original for *Invasion from Mars* (Dell).

1950

"The Dreaming Jewels," *Fantastic Adventures*, February.
"The Stars Are the Styx," *Galaxy*, November.

1951

"Rule of Three," *Galaxy*, January.
"Shadow, Shadow on the Wall," *Imagination*, February.
"Last Laugh" ("Special Aptitude"), *Other Worlds*, March.
"Make Room for Me," *Fantastic Adventures*, May.
"The Traveling Crag," *Fantastic Adventures*, July.
"Excalibur and the Atom," *Fantastic Adventures*, August.
"The Incubi of Parallel X," *Planet Stories*, September.

1952

"Never Underestimate," *If*, March.
"Baby Is Three," *Galaxy*, October.
"The Sex Opposite," *Fantastic*, Fall.

1953

"Saucer of Loneliness," *Galaxy*, February.
"The World Well Lost," *Universe Science Fiction*, June.
"And My Fear Is Great," *Beyond*, July.
"The Wages of Synergy," *Startling Stories*, August.
"The Dark Room," *Fantastic*, August.
"Talent," *Beyond*, September.
"The Touch of Your Hand," *Galaxy*, September.
"A Way of Thinking," *Amazing*, November.
"The Silken Swift," *Fantasy and Science Fiction*, November.
"Mr. Costello, Hero," *Galaxy*, December.
"The Clinic," original for *Star Science Fiction #2*, Ballantine.
"The Fabulous Idiot," "Morality," originals for *More Than Human*, Ballantine.

1954

"The Education of Drusilla Strange," *Galaxy*, March.
"Beware the Fury" ("Extrapolation"), *Fantastic*, April.
"Granny Won't Knit," *Galaxy*, May.
"The Golden Helix," *Thrilling Wonder Stories*, Summer.
"Cactus Dance," *Luke Short's Western*, October-November.

"To Here and the Easel," original for *Star Short Novels*, Ballantine.

1955

"When You're Smiling," *Galaxy*, January.

"Who?," *Galaxy*, March.

"Hurricane Trio," *Galaxy*, April.

"The Heart," *Other Worlds*, May.

"Riddle of Ragnorak" (with Don Ward), *Fantastic Universe*, June.

"Twink," *Galaxy*, August.

"So Near the Darkness," *Fantastic Universe*, November.

"The (Widget), the (Wadget) and Boff," *Fantasy and Science Fiction* (in two parts), November and December issues.

1956

"Won't You Walk?," *Astounding Science Fiction*, January.

"The Skills of Xanadu," *Galaxy*, July.

"Claustrophile," *Galaxy*, August.

"Fear Is a Business," *Fantasy and Science Fiction*, August.

"The Other Man," *Galaxy*, September.

"And Now the News," *Fantasy and Science Fiction*, December.

1957

"The Girl Had Guts," *Venture Science Fiction*, January.

"The Other Celia," *Galaxy*, March.

"Affair With a Green Monkey," *Venture Science Fiction*, May.

"The Pod in the Barrier," *Galaxy*, September.

"It Opens the Sky," *Venture Science Fiction*, November.

1958

"A Touch of Strange," *Fantasy and Science Fiction*, January.

"The Comedian's Children," *Venture Science Fiction*, May.

"To Marry Medusa," *Galaxy*, August.

1959

"The Man Who Lost the Sea," *Fantasy and Science Fiction*, October.

1960

"Like Young," *Fantasy and Science Fiction*, March.

"Need," original for *Beyond*, Avon.

1961

"Tandy's Story," *Galaxy*, April.

1962

"When You Care, When You Love," *Fantasy and Science Fiction*, September.

1964

"How to Forget Baseball," *Sports Illustrated*, December 21.

1965

"The Nail and the Oracle," *Playboy*, October.

CHAD OLIVER

He's a big wide-shouldered Texas-tall man who smiles often, is hard on himself and gentle with others. He enjoys the direct verbal challenge of a college class-room, and students respond to his wit, his natural ease, the unquestioned knowledge behind what he tells them.

In science fiction, though it sometimes discomforts him to recall the fact, he began as a rabid fan, a prolific letter-writer of awesome intensity. In the old days, when almost every science fiction magazine had a letter column, Oliver filled them. He raved, criticized, congratulated authors, rated stories, inserted puns, bemoaned cover illustrations. Yet his boyish enthusiasm was tempered with sound story judgment; his wild wit was leavened with serious suggestions as to the im-provement of the genre. He was a buff, an aficionado, a True Believer.

It was inevitable, therefore, that when Chad Oliver began to write professionally his efforts were science-fictional, combining his study of anthropology with his basic sympathy for and awareness of the human condi-tion. Chad was, then, that rare and welcome fellow, the practical dreamer; his fiction was rooted in hard science, but the tendrils of his creative imagination thrust out to the stars.

He was born in Cincinnati, Ohio, in 1928—and grew up digging jazz and football and pulp magazines. He soon became a Texan, and now it is difficult to think of him as anything else. His family lived in Crys-tal City, and Chad learned to ride, acquired a lasting affection for the vast lands, the winds and skies, prairies and canyons of this sprawling state. He has become an expert in the history of the Plains Indian, and some of his best work utilizes this expansive historical background: stories in *Argosy* and *Saturday Evening Post* —and a splendidly realized novel, *The Wolf Is My Brother*.

He was twenty-two when he sold his first story, "The Boy Next Door," to Anthony Boucher, then editing *Fantasy and Science Fiction.** Martha Foley cited it that season for her "Distinctive Short Stories in American Magazines," a signal honor for a beginning writer.

Boucher wrote of him, "Oliver is a prime contender for the Heinlein-Clarke front rank of genuine science fiction, in which the science is as accurately absorbing as the fiction is richly human."

Chad's offbeat humor and a broad sense of the absurd often thread his work; during an informal radio interview he was asked, quite seriously, where he'd met his wife. Chad politely replied, "In the science lab at college. I was going to the cabinet to obtain some rare bone specimens. I pulled out a big drawer and there she was."

I met him in 1953, when he was in California studying for his Ph.D. in anthropology at U.C.L.A. (He had already earned B.A. and M.A. degrees from the University of Texas.) Forry Ackerman was then agenting Chad's science fiction work, as he was mine. I was still a year away from my first sale and eager to learn the secrets of professional science fiction. I found, in Chad's stories, a natural warmth which intrigued me. The man himself matched it, and his wife, Beje (or BJ—for Betty Jane) was equally delightful. We all became close friends.

The Olivers eventually rented a small, rustic wooden cabin perched high on a dirt ledge in the Bel Air Hills—and the regular group who gathered there included the Charles Beaumonts and the Richard Mathe-

* As the index shows, two other stories appeared first in *Super Science* due to Boucher's inability to schedule the story before June of 1951.

sons. Even then, as I recall, Chad was busily mapping out a trip to British East Africa to study the lives of the Kamba, the third largest native tribe in Kenya. Armed with a smattering of Swahili and a dozen inoculations against assorted fevers, he and Beje arrived there in 1961, beginning a productive year in the rugged Hemingway brush country.

I have an Oliver letter sent from Africa, in which he stated, "In many areas the Kamba still carry bows and poisoned arrows which are used to protect them from the raids of the Masai, who live on the great flat plains to the southwest. . . . Elephants are considered *the* most dangerous animals over here, since they frequently smash in the windshields of cars and drag the luckless occupants out to stamp on them. I was in the Land Rover, fighting the dirt road, when I cleared a hairpin turn to encounter a big bull elephant surrounded by yelling Kambas who were trying to puncture his hide from a distance with their poisoned arrows. The elephant charged my Rover, but I managed to get around him and continue on to Mbooni. . . . There was nothing left but the bones when I came back down the road that evening. . . . The Kamba are a hungry people."

And later Chad wrote, "We have settled down to an easy routine, the monotony broken occasionally by such minor incidents as BJ being charged by a two-ton rhino . . . by one of our crew suffering an attack of maggots in his back . . . and the morning at breakfast when a newborn bat dropped out of the rafters into our porridge. . . . Then it began to rain: seventeen inches in the first three days. The rain lasted through November —more than it had rained in one hundred years in Kenya! Bridges were washed away; all the dirt roads became seas of mud. Our water supply failed, and we drank from the sky. Food had to be dropped in by plane—but we're drying out now, and the work goes on."

The result of that year's study: a Kamba monograph and an African novel which Chad is still polishing. He's back in Texas now, as Professor Oliver, teaching anthropology at the University of Texas, having recently bought an eight-acre spread with "the regular assortment of horses and pigs."

Chad once conducted his own weekly hour-long disc jockey show out of KHFI in Austin, devoted to jazz classics. (He plays drums and piano.) Football, poker, pipe-smoking, Colorado trout fishing and his daughter Kim are all Oliver passions, along with the poetry of A. E. Housman—which has inspired some of his best stories.

He's been in two dozen anthologies, including many "Bests," and his science fiction novel, *Shadows in the Sun,* was cited by *The New York Times* as tops in its field for that year.

Anthropology continues to fascinate him, and he has said of it, "The human mind is a time machine that can carry us backward or forward at will. . . . The average anthropologist, in his study of groups and cultures, moves back in time. If he writes science fiction, he may also move *forward,* into an imagined future, using man's history as a base. Anthropology is a young science, as sciences go, but it is a very important one, for if we are to survive in a world of atomic energy and warring nations we must learn to know one another. That's what anthropology is all about—the study of man as a physical and cultural animal."

In his powerful, beautifully structured novella, "The Marginal Man," we share an interstellar adventure on an alien world in a typical Oliver blend of science and imagination. Here is a story which examines "the relation between technological man and primitive man, and the ultimate definition of civilization."

THE MARGINAL MAN
Chad Oliver

I

The small gray metallic sphere drifted down through the night sky of Pollux V twenty-nine light-years from Earth. The eerie pinkish glow of the two moons glinted softly on the floating sphere against its backdrop of silver stars. Already, invisibly far out in space, the ion drive of the mother ship from Earth's CAS fleet had flared into life again, carrying the great ship back into the lonely darkness between the worlds.

The sphere was alone.

It dropped gently through the atmosphere on its antigravs toward the dark surface of the planet below. It made no sound, drifting through the strange moonlight as insubstantially as a ghost from some forgotten world. It hovered above the branches of a stand of trees for a moment, shifted course slightly, and settled in a field of grass and shrubs. It barely disturbed the grass at first and then, as the antigravs shut off, it crushed into the ground with its true weight.

A circular port slid open and two men stepped out. The light from inside the sphere beamed through the port and mixed with the rose of the moonlight. The two men were clearly visible and made no effort to conceal themselves.

Even physically, the two men were a contrast and their first actions on the unknown world merely underlined the differences between them. Arthur Canady, tall and lean and dour, leaned back against the side of the sphere and lit his pipe with hardly a glance at the new world around him. Frank Landis scurried around like a newly released puppy, his stocky body scuttling back and forth between dimly glimpsed rocks and shrubs and night-blooming flowers, his sandy hair like a feverish halo over his open, eager face.

"Look at this, Art," he said, retrieving a delicate white flower that looked like an orchid. "How about that? Isn't it something?"

Arthur Canady puffed on his pipe solemnly. "I knew a man once who ate flowers," he said.

"Why'd he do that?" Frank asked, falling into the trap as usual.

"To get to the other side," Arthur Canady explained patiently.

Frank Landis looked at him blankly. "Sometimes I just don't get you, Art."

"I'm not always contagious, I guess."

"I mean, what the *hell*. Here we are, the first civilized men ever to set foot on a new world—it's an historic moment—and you're not even interested."

"I wouldn't say that," Canady said, uncoiling himself from the side of the sphere. "It's just that botany is a little out of my line. For instance, unless you're too set on making a little speech about the Mission from Earth and the Great Terran Father, I suspect that there's something important going on over there right now that we ought to see." He pointed toward the west.

Frank looked and saw nothing. "What's over there?"

"Among other things, if our survey map is accurate, there's a good-sized stream. On the banks of that stream, the natives have a camp—a big one. And they're having a ceremony of some sort."

"What makes you think so?"

"See that glow over there, through those trees? Unless you happen to believe in a horde of giant lightning bugs, that means a series of large fires. And if you'll turn up your hearing aid a bit you can hear what sounds like a chant of some kind. Tired hunters aren't very apt to be just practicing their harmony around the old campfire, so I assume there is some type of ceremony going on. And I think we ought to be there."

"Now?" Frank asked.

"Why not?"

Frank stared at his companion. He had never worked with Canady before and knew him only by his reputation. Dammit, no matter how good an anthropologist he might be, the man wasn't *comfortable*.

"You're not afraid of a few hundred natives, are you?" Canady asked, smiling.

"Of course not! I'm sure you know what you're doing. It's just that—well, we just got here—seems like rushing it a bit . . ."

Canady tapped his pipe out against his boot, carefully smothering the hot ashes with dirt. He had rather suspected that Frank, for all his too-frequent sermons about his love for primitive peoples, preferred to deal with natives from a position of massive strength. Well, he had a point there and this was no time to start a silly argument. "Don't worry, Frank. We'll wait until tomorrow and run through the customary contact routines. I'm just going to sneak over there and have a look through the glasses. You can stay here if you like."

He got his glasses out of the sphere, locating them under Frank's demonstration steam engine, and stuck a pistol in his belt. Then, without another word, he struck off to the west toward the sound of the chanting. He would really have preferred to go alone, to savor this new world without the bubble-bath of Frank's somewhat shrill enthusiasms, but he hadn't gone fifty yards before Frank panted up behind him and fell into step.

"This is really something," Frank exclaimed. "I feel like Robinson Crusoe!"

Canady toyed with a vision of a suitable desert island but held his tongue. His long legs covered the ground with an easy, effortless stride. He felt rather than saw the lovely moons in the star-sprinkled sky, felt the alien wind in his lungs, felt the strange and

wonderful sounds and smells and impressions that
tugged oddly at his heart.

He entered the darkness beneath the trees, silent as
a shadow, and slipped toward the orange glow of the
firelight. The chanting was closer now; it had a weird
and haunting atonality to it, a subtle rhythm that was
hard to catch—

Canady quickened his steps, all thoughts of Frank
forgotten. There was a sadness in him, and a name-
less hunger.

Twenty-nine light-years from the planet Earth it
had begun again.

Hidden in a clump of thorny bushes on a low hill
overlooking the stream-cut valley, Arthur Canady held
the glasses to his eyes and stared down upon a scene
of wild magnificence, a scene that filled him with wonder and the sense of a life beyond his knowledge, a
life glimpsed far away, a life he could never enter.

It was something that the survey charts and the
planted microphones had not prepared him for. He was
a man who was seldom surprised but he was surprised
now. It was the difference between a faded photograph
and the reality, the difference between a set of statis-
tics and the miracle of human beings. All the expected
culture elements were there, but the *intensity* of the
thing was astonishing. And there was something
more . . .

The stream coursed through the moonlit valley, pink
and silver beneath the moons. Tremendous fires blazed
along the river banks, hissing and crackling with the
rich juices of fresh sap, shooting spectacular showers
of sparks high into the air. The orange glow of the
flames bathed the rows of tepee-like skin tents in lam-
bent, living light.

There must have been close to a thousand men and
women camped by the river, which was an amazing
number of people for a hunting culture. Every last
person was taking part in the ceremony: dancing, preparing food, singing. They were a tall, robust people;
they moved proudly with their heads held high. They

were dressed in a wild and barbaric splendor: fur robes and feathers and intricately painted designs on their graceful bodies.

The chanting was continuous. It was a joyful, happy kind of music, serving as a chorus behind the whirling forms of the dancers. Most primitive music, Canady had always felt, was just that: primitive and incredibly monotonous. But this was something else: a lively, complex wave of counterpoint and rhythm that set a man's blood racing in his veins. And the dancing was no mere shuffling of feet in a circle; it was abandoned and yet controlled, graceful as a ballet but with a rough sexuality to it that was strangely innocent, strangely pure.

The happiness and the joy were tangible things; you could feel them in the air. It was a time of rejoicing, a time of release, a time of thanksgiving. And yet there was a dark undercurrent to it, a shadow that moved in and out among the firelit dancers like a whisper of remorse. . . .

In the precise center of the camp one fire blazed higher than all the others. A constant stream of men fed fresh wood to it, tossing mighty logs into the flames. It was a hot, roaring fire, a pivot around which all else revolved. It drew the eye like a magnet.

The two men from Earth lay silent, watching. Both of them knew that they had a once-in-a-lifetime opportunity and they took full advantage of it. Tomorrow their work would begin, the work that would spell the end of the life they were watching, but for now it was only something to see, something to remember when the old days were gone.

The dancing and the chanting continued. It went on for hours, rising in intensity all the time. The dances grew wilder, the chanting rose to a climax that was almost unendurable. The fires blazed and the moons arced across the night sky, shaming the distant light of the stars.

When it happened, it happened with a startling abruptness.

The chanting stopped, as though cut off with a

switch. The dancers stopped in mid-step. The natives moved into a silent circle around the central fire. A hush fell over the night, a hush of expectancy. . . .

One man stepped out from the others, framed in the leaping flames. He was naked, free of ornament of any kind. He raised his right hand and then his left. He bowed to the four directions. He looked up, out into the night and the moons and the stars. His face was radiant with a supreme peace.

Calmly, without hesitation, he walked into the roaring fire.

He climbed up the searing logs, his hair already aflame. He lay down on his back on a bed of fire. He did not move. He did not cry out. His body disappeared in a mass of flame, even the bones lost in the red-hot coals that fed the fire.

The fire blazed higher, crackling and hissing.

It was done.

The natives turned silently and filed back to their tents by twos and threes. No one looked back at the funeral pyre. Within minutes there was not a human being to be seen anywhere. The stream wound through the valley, gliding smoothly in the fading light. The fires blazed for a remarkably short time, then died away into glowing coals. The great fire that had eaten a life was the last to go, flaring and sparking as though reluctant to give up its moment of splendor, but it finally faded and collapsed into a pile of smoking embers.

The night stole in again, covering the tents with darkness.

The two men from Earth eased themselves out of the concealing bushes and walked back under the stars to their waiting sphere. Even Frank had nothing to say.

Canady felt the strange world around him, felt it as a palpable presence, and was filled with an excitement that had no name. He felt that he stood on the edge of marvels, of wonders that dwelt in an abyss of dreams.

One thing he knew: this was no ordinary hunting culture, no matter what the survey charts showed.

He slept badly, impatient for the morning sun.

II

The sun was a red glory in the sky and by its harsh light the world of Pollux V lost much of its ethereal quality and resolved itself into a matter-of-fact land of rolling plains, distant mountains, and stands of tall trees that followed the river valleys. After a breakfast of concentrated coffee and powdered eggs, Canady found it difficult to recapture his mood of the night before. What he had seen *had* been unprecedented, but perhaps he had attached too much importance to it.

Still, it was odd. The man who had walked into the flames had seemed to do so of his own free will; he had not been forced. He had not been a sacrifice in the usual sense of the word, and in any event human sacrifices were normally a luxury restricted to higher types of culture with larger populations. The man had *wanted* to go into those flames. Why? And why had his death been the occasion for such rejoicing on the part of the rest of the people? There had certainly been more than one band present; people must have come in from miles around to share in the festivities. . . .

Canady shook his head. It was folly to speculate on such things until you knew enough about the culture to make sense of them. He put the incident from his mind and settled into routine.

And routine it was. The first contact between Earth and a primitive culture was always a dramatic event but the procedure was cut and dried. The scientists of Earth's Cultural Aid Service had worked out a plan for every known type of culture and all the field men had to do was to follow the proper plan in simple ABC fashion. All the plans, based on centuries of experience on Earth and on the nearer planetary systems, were designed to do two basic things: show the people that the newcomers were friendly, and show them that they were too powerful to be attacked. It was a neat example of the age-old technique of putting a big smile on your face and carrying a sharp knife in your toga.

While Frank set up his equipment in the sphere, Canady took a high-powered rifle and set out across the plains toward a small herd of grazing animals. The animals (called yedoma in the local native dialect) were large beasts that looked like the American moose, save that the horns on the males were short and stubby affairs like those of domestic cattle. The economic life of the natives—as best the CAS could gather from photographic and microphonic survey—was based on the herds of yedoma that roamed the plains; yedoma meat, fresh or dried, was the food staple, yedoma skins were used for tents and clothing, yedoma sinew was used for thread. It was a neat parallel to the reliance of the ancient Plains Indians upon the buffalo, and it offered an exceptionally easy situation for cultural manipulation.

Canady kept the wind in his face and it was a simple matter to get close enough to the herd for a shot. The animals had had no experience with a weapon that killed at long range and were aware of no danger. Canady dropped a yedoma calf with one shot and could easily have killed half the herd if there had been any point in it. He dragged the calf back to the sphere and lifted it inside.

They were ready.

Frank Landis took the controls and lifted the sphere into the morning sky with the effortless ease of a man to whom all things mechanical were second nature. There was little sensation of movement within the sphere as it floated over the plain toward the native camp.

Canady sat quietly, smoking his pipe. It was crowded inside the sphere, crowded with portable steam engines and sacks of seeds and repeating firearms and that greatest of all invasion threats, crates of sewing machines. He thought of the wild and free scene the night before, the tents and the fires and the dancing, and he thought of it as a way of life already gone, destroyed by the bland deadliness of sacks of seeds and crates of sewing machines. The old regret saddened him, and he was unable to comfort himself by the neat-sounding official phrases that cloaked the operation of the Cultural Aid Service.

In theory, they were helping the natives. The fact that the natives had asked for no help was not mentioned. The speeches at the United Nations were fairly dripping with high-sounding phrases about underdeveloped areas, primitive misery, and the moral obligation of the strong to help the weak. There was much oratory about starving children and the glorious benefits of civilization.

Behind the scenes, oddly enough, much of the talk was along the same lines. All men wear cultural blinkers which condition them to curiously inevitable chains of reasoning. Given certain premises, certain conclusions follow as certainly as fish swallow worms. The goals and aspirations of a man's own culture just naturally seem *right* for all other cultures as well, and surely you are doing the other fellow a service by passing on the joys that you yourself have known. . . .

And then, of course, there *was* the fact that primitive areas make poor markets for an industrial civilization. The development of the ion drive had made trade commercially sound, and Earth's factories were not geared to mass-produce arrow points. If you want to sell a man a tri-di set, it helps to have electricity first. If you want to sell a man a tractor, it is nice if agriculture has already been invented. If you're thinking in terms of consumers, a large and prosperous population is better than a small and poverty-stricken one.

The human mind is infinitely capable of rationalization; it can justify anything from crusades to slavery on the basis of Good, Pure, and Noble Motives.

Canady had never considered himself a romantic man. He was a product of his culture and he had to live in it. He had found a job that interested him, a job that offered good pay and prestige, and he did his job honestly. But he had never been able to convince himself that he was a knight in shining armor by reciting a string of platitudes. He was too wise a man to believe that he could change the universe by a one-man fight against injustice, so he simply did what men have always done—he did the best he could to ease some of the pain along the way.

Right now, as the sphere floated over the treetops, he was not unduly proud of himself. Even the argument that he was gaining valuable data for his science failed to reassure him, and it was a mark of his honesty that he did not even consider the argument that if he didn't do the job somebody else would.

Frank looked up from the controls, his blue eyes disturbed. He was not an insensitive man and many of the same thoughts had been bothering him. Frank, however, could always sell himself on the rightness of what he was doing. It was not dishonesty on his part; his brain just worked that way.

"Seems kind of a shame," he said. "I guess they like their life pretty well the way it is."

"Maybe not," Canady said, helping him out. "After all, Frank, that's an argument that might have kept us all in the caves."

"That's right." Frank's eyes brightened. "Hell, if you don't believe in *progress,* what can you believe in?"

Canady could think of several answers to that one but he just shrugged as though the problem were insoluble. The blind faith in progress—which normally, if you tried to pin it down to anything approaching preciseness, meant increased technological complexity —was so deeply ingrained in Earth's cultures that it had become an automatic response. Even children believed in progress. How could you not believe in progress?

"I look at it this way," Frank said slowly. "We're taking something away from them, sure. We're asking them to change their way of life on a purely voluntary basis—we're not *forcing* them to do anything. In return, we're offering them things they've never had before: comfort and good health and security. What's wrong with that?"

"Your insight is very comforting," Canady said without smiling. "Got the bomb ready?"

Frank looked at him sharply, disturbed by the juxta-position of the two sentences. Canady, however, smoked his pipe without expression. "It's ready."

Canady studied the terrain below in the viewers. They were over a cleared area near the native camp. He checked the safety detectors. There were no people in the target area, but it was close enough so that they could get an eyeful.

"Let go the convincer," he said.

Frank tripped the switch and the bomb fell. It went off with a satisfying bang and set off a cloud of smoke out of all proportion to any damage it might have done. It was not atomic, of course. There was no need to use a block-buster when a firecracker would serve.

"Set her down," he said.

Frank jockeyed the sphere into position above the rows of skin tents and landed it in the precise center of the camp. They waited until the natives had had time to form a cautious circle around them and then they opened the port.

The two men from Earth stepped out, smiles on their faces and their right hands raised in gestures of peace.

Canady's troubled green eyes took in the whole works with one swift, experienced glance. Anthropologists who have spent long years in the field tend to be more impressed with the similarities between cultures than with their obvious differences. It is only the un-trained eye that seizes upon the somewhat superficial oddities and cannot see beyond the seemingly bizarre to the deeply rooted universals that underlie all human social systems. A nomadic hunting culture *has* to have certain characteristics for the excellent reason that it will work in no other way. This, as Canady was well aware, is just as true twenty-nine light-years from Earth as it was in aboriginal Asia, Africa, or North America. A scientific law is binding no matter where you find it.

He saw a great deal in that one quick check. He saw not only the scene before him but saw it projected against a backdrop of facts and figures, saw it neatly divided up into familiar categories. Even if he had not already known a great deal about the natives from the planted microphones that had enabled him to learn the language, he could have predicted rather closely what these people would be like. Now as always in the moment of initial contact, he was on the alert for anything off-key, anything that didn't fit. It was the unexpected that could make for trouble.

At first, he saw nothing unusual.

The natives stood in a loose circle, waiting. There were fewer of them now than there had been the night before; obviously the other bands had dispersed after the ceremony. Canady estimated the crowd at about sixty-five men and women. They were a tall, healthy-looking group with that robustness of bone and muscle that comes from an outdoor life and a predominantly meat diet. The men were dressed in skin leggings and had ornate bone combs stuck into their long dark hair. The women wore a simple skin tunic, tied at the waist with beaded thongs.

Canady spotted his first oddity: none of the natives was carrying a weapon of any kind. He filed the fact away.

Canady lowered his hand. "We visit The People in peace," he said loudly in the native language. "We come among The People as friends. We come from the sky to bring honor to the Old Ones and many gifts to The People."

Precisely on cue, Frank dragged the yedoma calf out of the sphere and placed it on the ground before the natives. There was a low murmur from the people. A man stepped forward, his dark bronzed skin glistening in the sun. He was dressed exactly like the rest except that his head-comb was blue rather than white. He raised his right hand. "You are welcome among The People," he said quietly. "We thank you for your gift. Our food is your food, and our camp your camp."

It was all according to formula but Canady felt again the stirrings of uneasiness. The natives were too calm, too self-assured. Surely the bomb had had *some* effect. . . .

"We bring not only friendship to The People," he said. "We bring many useful gifts to make your days easier. We bring a hunting stick that kills with a sound like thunder."

Frank stepped out again with a repeating rifle in his hand. He lifted the weapon to his shoulder, took aim on a small tree, and fired six shots in rapid succession. The trunk of the tree splintered neatly and a fragment of bark fell to the ground. The staccato sound of the shots died away and there was silence.

The natives watched impassively, giving him their courteous attention. They were neither frightened nor impressed.

Canady finished his speech rather lamely. "It is our hope that this day will mark the beginning of a long friendship between The People and our own people. It is our hope that the Old Ones will look with favor upon our visit, and that we may each learn many things."

The native with the blue comb nodded. He waited to make sure that Canady had finished speaking, and then stepped forward and took his arm. He smiled, showing fine, even teeth. "Come," he said. "You must be tired and hungry after your journey through the sky. Let us eat of the yedoma and talk to one another as men."

Canady hesitated, more and more unsure of himself. The *tone* of the thing was completely wrong. It was not that the natives were unfriendly, but there was certainly none of the usual gods-from-the-sky business. It was almost as though The People had visitors from space every day in the week. He looked at Frank out of the corner of his eye. Frank was smiling, still playing the Great White Father role.

"Bring the rifle," he said in English.

The native turned and led the way toward his splendidly painted tent. Canady and Frank walked along behind him. The native men and women watched them with no great interest and then went about their business.

"Well, I'll be damned," Canady said.

"This is really something," Frank whispered.

"It's something right enough," Canady agreed. "But what the devil *is* it?"

He followed the native into the tent, and he sensed once more that he stood on the edge of marvels, of wonders that dwelt in an abyss of dreams. . . .

The days that followed were easily the strangest of Canady's life. Psychologically, it is never a simple matter for a man to be uprooted from all that is familiar to him and set down in a way of life that is not his own. Previously, though, in his work in the Alpha Centauri system, Canady had at least been supported by the knowledge that his task was going well, that the situation was fully under control. And Dave, who had shared those years with him, had been much more of a friend than Frank Landis could ever be.

Canady had never felt so utterly alone. Even in his troubled adolescence in New Chicago he had had understanding parents who gave him an anchor in a bustling world. Later, there had been a series of women—though he had never married—and the quiet contentment of summers in the unspoiled national forests of Colorado. His interest in his work had sustained him when all else failed, and now even his confidence in his knowledge was shaken.

It was made all the more difficult by the fact that there was nothing wrong with The People that he could put his finger on. There were no signposts erected in the village that advertised BIG MYSTERY HERE. The People were friendly enough in their fashion and they were more than willing to cooperate. They did all the things that they were supposed to do. The men rode out of the camp on their camel-like mharus in hunting parties, searching for the grazing herds of yedoma which they brought down with their bows and arrows. The women cooked and worked long hours in preparing skins and gathering wild plants from the river valleys. Often, at night while the two moons sailed among the stars, stories were told around the campfires, stories of the Old Ones and the Long Walk and the heroic deeds of the warriors of The People.

It was all very normal on the surface. But the nuances were all wrong, completely beyond Canady's understanding. The grace notes of the culture were subtly alien in a way he could not fathom. Frank was merely puzzled and a little hurt by the reception given to his bag of tricks, but Canady was deeply disturbed.

He tried to drive a wedge of understanding into the culture by falling back on the most reliable of all techniques. He began by employing the genealogical method, a safe introductory gambit for centuries. He sat down with Plavgar, the blue-combed native who seemed to have the high status of a headman. He asked him all the innocuous, surefire questions. What was the name of his wife? What had been the names of her parents? What had been the names of his parents? What were the names of their children, if any? This sort of thing was practically guaranteed to set any native off on a long chain of reminiscences about his family for generations back, and in the process the anthropologist could gain a valuable key to the various kinship connections that were so important in a primitive society. Plavgar, however, simply did not respond. He gave his wife's name, and explained that she had been obtained by raiding a neighboring band. He gave the name of his father and mother—and then proceeded to name almost everyone in the band, calling them all father and mother, and offering to introduce them to Canady. The idea of brothers and sisters appeared to puzzle him. As for generations past, he was a complete blank. Since peoples without a means of writing always made a point of remembering relatives to a really amazing degree, this was manifestly impossible.

He did get a typical culture hero story, about a man who had led an almost legendary mharu raid against the Telliomata, swiping their entire mharu herd from right under their eyes. But then Plavgar blandly offered to introduce Canady to the culture hero, who could be seen at that moment calmly gnawing on a steak in front of his tepee.

Frank set up his steam engine and showed The People the work it could do. They watched the demonstration politely, as one might watch a child putting together a model airplane, and then ignored it. Frank got out his battery-powered sewing machines and played his trump card. He took the women aside and showed them how they could cut their work-day in half. The women tried it out, smiling and eager to please, and then went back to their bone needles.

Even the rifles, so demonstrably superior to the native bows and arrows, failed to have the desired effect. The natives admired Frank's shooting and that was all. This was a serious business, because the rifle was a lever that the men from Earth had relied heavily upon. Once you substituted rifles for bows in a hunting culture you had a ready-made market. Not only would the natives become so dependent on the rifles that they would in time forget how to make bows, but the introduction of the rifle would set off a chain reaction that would completely upset the balance of power between the native groups. A band with rifles was unbeatable. Then, the mere threat of taking the rifles away or withholding ammunition was all the threat you needed. . . .

Try as he might, Canady could get no information about shamans. At first, he put this down to an understandable tabu against referring to the supernatural. But the natives did not shy away from his questions: they simply assured him that they didn't *have* any curers or healers or medicine men. He got a lot of patient talk about the Old Ones, and that was that. He shook his head. He had never heard of a primitive culture without shamans—it was as unthinkable as a copter without an atmosphere. What did they do when they got sick?

It was not until he had been on the planet for two full months that the truth hit him in the face, the truth that should have been obvious from the first. It was so simple, so utterly out in the open, that its significance had completely escaped him. And it was so fantastic that the very idea was automatically rejected by the mind.

It all began when Lerrie, the wife of Rownar, announced that she was pregnant.

III

A fever pitch of excitement ran through the camp of The People and Canady found himself caught up in it despite himself. He had lived long enough to know that true happiness was the rarest of all gifts and the natives around him were almost delirious with joy. Even the certain knowledge that he was on the verge of a tremendous scientific discovery paled to insignificance. There was a smile on every face and work was impossible. A sense of miraculous well-being permeated the very air. It was a holiday mood and Canady surrendered to it.

The People had stayed long in one place and it was time to move on. The warm summer months were fading into the chill of autumn and the yedoma herds were migrating to the south across the grassy, rolling plains. The People would have had to follow them in any case, but it was definitely the news about Lerrie that triggered their departure.

The great tents were struck and the hides were lashed to pack mharus. The tent poles were tied to the flanks of the beasts so that their tips dragged along the ground. The tips were securely lashed together, travois-fashion, to form a V-shaped platform upon which The People placed their few belongings. The men and women mounted their mharus and they were ready. Leaving home was as simple as that.

The People moved out at dawn on a cold, gray day. A light rain was falling and the yedoma robes were welcome against their shoulders. Canady, moved by an impulse he hardly understood, rode with the natives. His camel-like mharu was a spirited mount and he felt oddly at peace on the scrap of hide that served as a saddle. His tall, lean body had grown hard in his months with The People and the wind-swept rain in his face was fresh and cool, the breath of life itself.

Dammit, he thought, *I feel like a man again.*

Frank followed along behind the tribe, piloting the sphere. He held it just above the level of the grass and its soundless presence was curiously unreal. The People ignored it and whenever Canady glanced back and saw it hovering over the plain behind him he felt a wild urge to laugh. The thing was somehow comical, for all the engineering skill that had gone into it. When compared with the magnificent vitality of the world around it the sphere became a kind of cipher, colorless and blatantly trivial. It seemed to sail along in a void, trying without success to attract attention to itself. It was a loud-shirted tourist in a forest of cool pines and it didn't matter, it was overwhelmed. . . .

A day and a night and a day The People rode. They did not seem to hurry and they dozed in their saddles and chewed on dried meat and berries as they traveled but there was a definite direction to their wandering. They crossed the windy plains and struck a trail that wound up into the foothills of a range of purple, snow-capped mountains. They rode into a sheltered canyon where a small stream trickled out of a glacial spring, a canyon where the trees were tall and dark and green. They moved through the evening shadows, pitching their tents and building great yellow fires that warmed the chill air.

Canady was sore and red-eyed from lack of sleep. The trick of dozing in the saddle looked easy enough when the natives did it, but he had discovered that the jerky gait of the mharu was anything but soothing. He decided that perhaps the rugged outdoor life was not an unalloyed joy after all and stumbled into the sphere with relief. The warm, dry bunk pulled him like a magnet and he fell into it without bothering to take off his damp, dirt-streaked clothes.

Frank, neat and clean and freshly shaven, wrinkled his nose. "You smell like a fertilizer factory, my friend," he said. "Remember, I live here too."

"Make yourself at home," Canady said. He yawned, too tired to argue. "Call me early, will you? I have a feeling that something's going to pop, and I don't want to miss it."

Frank said something else, then looked more closely at his companion and gave up. Canady was already snoring lustily. Frank smiled and managed to haul off the sleeping man's boots, which he held at arm's length and deposited outside on the ground. He gently placed a blanket over Canady's body and sat down to write up his field notes for the day.

He shook his head. Canady was a funny guy.

Outside in the night, a single voice was raised in a plaintive chant. It was a woman's voice, soft and lovely in the silence. Frank listened to it for a long time and then he too went to bed.

The woman chanted on, her voice liquid and true, and it was hard to tell whether it was a song she sang, or a prayer. . . .

The next day dawned clear and cold with a thin wind whining down from the mountain snows. The sheltered valley, dark with tall fir trees, was slow to warm and the tepees of The People stood like frozen sentinels on the canyon floor.

Arthur Canady stood surveying the scene, his long legs wide apart, his work-roughened hands on his hips. There was a respectable black beard on his face and he had let his hair grow long. He shivered a little in the cold and tried to determine his next move. There was no doubt that they had failed utterly in their mission to date; the natives had shown no interest at all in the fancy gadgets they had brought from Earth. This didn't bother Canady—in fact it gave him a secret satisfaction—but what did bother him was the fact that after months with The People he was still a stranger. He felt a keen sense of not belonging, of being an outsider. He had made no friends and this had never happened to him before. The People were not hostile and they treated him with every courtesy, but they did not *accept* him.

That hurt.

He walked along the line of tepees, smelling the rich odors of yedoma steaks broiling over the cookfires. He saw Lerrie, the wife of Rownar, washing her face in the cold waters of the mountain stream. She looked up at him and smiled. She looked radiantly beautiful as though filled with an inner joy that stamped itself upon her every feature. Her eyes sparkled in the morning sunlight. She shook the water from her face and began to comb out her long black hair.

"Good morning," he said.

"It is a lovely morning, Ar-thur." It was odd to hear his name on her lips and the sound of his name took on a strange music.

"The Old Ones have been kind," he said, following the formula. "I rejoice for you."

She smiled again. "I am to be a mother," she said, as though this were the most wonderful thing in the world. "I, Lerrie, am to have a child!"

"That is good." Canady hesitated, searching for the right words, "It is your first?" he asked.

She stared at him and then laughed aloud. "My first! Surely you are joking with me? Of course it is my first. How could it be otherwise?"

"Forgive me; many of your customs are still strange to me. Lerrie, in my world it is sometimes dangerous to ask a woman how old she is. Do you mind if I ask you? How old are you, Lerrie?"

She frowned as though puzzled. "How . . . *old*?"

"How many seasons have you lived?"

She shook her head. "I do not know," she said simply. "We do not count such things. I am alive. That is all."

"Many seasons?" Canady persisted.

"Yes, Ar-thur. Many seasons."

"Do you remember when you were a child, Lerrie?"

She pursed her lips. "It was long ago. I remember little." Her face brightened. "I do remember the Coming of Age, when I became one of The People. I will never forget that. I was so frightened. I had heard stories of the Long Walk, even then." She paused. "My child will be a good child, Ar-thur. He will have a good heart."

"I'm sure he will, Lerrie." He looked at the woman before him. She was hardly more than a girl. By Earthly standards she could not have been more than twenty-five years old. And yet she could not remember her childhood.

She had lived—how long?

Many seasons.

"I rejoice for you," he said again, and walked on to find Plavgar, the headman of The People. He found him sitting cross-legged in his tepee while his wife busied herself mending clothing. Canady was invited inside and seated himself on Plavgar's right, which he knew was proper etiquette for a guest. He said nothing until Plavgar's comely wife had served him a wooden bowlful of stew, which he dutifully sampled.

"Please smoke if you wish," Plavgar said. "I have noticed that it makes you more comfortable."

Canady pulled out his pipe, filled it, and lit it with a burning stick from the fire. The inside of the tepee was surprisingly roomy and spotlessly clean. The ground was covered with yedoma skins and the air smelled sweet and fresh. Canady took his time, puffing on his pipe. Plavgar sat quietly, watching him. He was a man of great dignity but except for the blue comb in his hair there was nothing about him to show his office of leader. He was still a young man in the prime of life, and yet his bearing was that of a man who had lived long and thought of many things.

"May I ask you some questions?" Canady said slowly.

Plavgar smiled. "That is your custom."

Canady flushed faintly. "I am sincere in wanting to know about The People. There are many things that I do not understand. As I stay with you longer, I find that I know less and less."

"That is the beginning of wisdom, my son." It was the first time that Plavgar had ever called him son and it pleased Canady. Of course, he himself was thirty-five, older than Plavgar looked, but the term seemed fitting.

"Do I have your permission to ask you anything I wish?"

Plavgar nodded, a faint twinkle in his eyes. "We have no secrets. I will help you all I can."

Canady leaned forward. "What happens to the children of The People?" he asked.

Plavgar frowned. "What happens to them? Why, they grow up into adult members of the tribe."

"They *always* grow up into adult members of the tribe?"

"Almost always. When a child is born he must learn many things. He must live among The People and learn their ways. If he has a good heart, he is sent out alone to Thunder Rock, high in the mountains. There he fasts for four days and there the Old Ones send a guardian spirit to him. He sees the guardian spirit and they become one. Then he goes through the Coming of Age, and he is one of The People forever."

"And if he does *not* have a good heart?"

"That does not often happen, my son. If he does not have a good heart, if he does not believe in the ways of The People, then the Old Ones are sad and will not accept him. His guardian spirit does not come to Thunder Rock and he is alone. If he has no guardian spirit, it would be unthinkable for him to take part in the Coming of Age."

"What happens to him?"

"He takes the Long Walk."

"You mean—he is expelled from the tribe?"

"He was never one of The People. He takes the Long Walk alone. He is alone forever or until his heart is good. A man cannot be a man until his heart is good."

Canady kept his face expressionless. His profession had taught him patience, if nothing else. It was always like this: the answers freely given that explained nothing. The guardian spirit complex was a familiar one, of course; it was the idea of a personal vision that came after fasting, a contact with the supernatural that gave a man a kind of personal phantom ally that accompanied him through life. If you were told throughout your childhood that you would see a spirit on Thunder Rock, and if you went without eating for four days alone in the mountains, you would see a spirit right enough. Particularly if you could not gain admission into the adult status in the tribe if you did *not* see a spirit. Still—

"I have heard much of the Old Ones. Can you tell me about them?"

"The Old Ones lived in the world before men came," Plavgar said, as though instructing a small child. "They were mighty beings and they live still in the high places. We cannot see them in our day-to-day life, but they are always there. They show themselves to us on Thunder Rock if we have a good heart. The Old Ones watch over our people and protect us from harm. The lives of the Old Ones and those of The People are one. We live together in harmony, and each is a part of the other."

That tells me exactly nothing, Canady thought.

He tried to bring the conversation down to a more concrete level. "Why is it that I have seen no children among The People?" he asked.

Plavgar smiled. "They have all grown up, The children are The People now."

Swell.

"And Lerrie?"

"The Old Ones have been kind. We rejoice for her, and we are thankful to Mewenta." Plavgar eyed him shrewdly. "You will stay with us long, my son?"

"Perhaps." The mother ship was due to pick them up twenty-two terrestrial months from now.

"Then you shall see for yourself what happens to the children of The People." Plavgar's face glowed. It seemed to be impossible for any native to refer to the coming child without a kind of inner ecstasy. "The Old Ones have been kind!"

"I rejoice with you," Canady said politely. There was a question nagging at him, something about what Plavgar had said. He tried to put his finger on it and failed. There were so many strange things—

He stood up. "I thank you for your time, Plavgar."

"I hope I have helped you," the headman said.

I hope so too, Canady thought, feeling far from certain.

He took his leave and went back to the sphere to dictate the text of his conversation with Plavgar and Lerrie.

All that afternoon, while Frank was busy trying to interest someone in his sewing machines, Canady puzzled over the data he had obtained. He felt that he had at least made some progress: he could pinpoint the areas in the culture that were causing the trouble. He could ask the right questions, and he knew that the answers were only a matter of time.

He smoked his pipe thoughtfully and as he worked he sensed a growing excitement within him. Approached solely as a puzzle, The People were more intriguing than any culture he had ever encountered. And if his hunch was right—

Looked at on a superficial level there was nothing at all extraordinary about The People. They formed a small hunting society based on the yedoma, they lived in tepees, they told stories about the Old Ones and believed in personal guardian spirits. There was nothing obviously wrong. But—

Item: None of the Earth's techniques for manipulating the culture had had the slightest effect. The culture was stable beyond belief. They not only had no interest in technology as such—they actively opposed any technological change. They wanted to keep their way of life the way it was. This was frequently the case in areas like social organization and religion, but Canady had never heard of a group that would not take to firearms and sewing machines like ducks to water. It was as though The People *knew* that the introduction of new technological elements would inevitably change their total way of life.

Item: Lerrie looked like a young girl. Yet she could not remember her childhood. She had no idea how old she was. And the notion of having more than one child had struck her as being ridiculous.

Item: There were no old individuals among The People. Canady had not seen a single person who looked over thirty. Even the leaders like Plavgar were young men.

Item: There were no children among The People. At first, Canady could hardly credit this, but there could be no doubt of it now. There were no babies, no adolescent boys and girls. Lerrie's pregnancy was a great event. Her child would be the only one in the tribe. . . .

Item: There were no shamans. There were no techniques for dealing with sickness.

What did it all add up to?

Suddenly, Canady remembered the phrase of Plavgar's that had troubled him when he first heard it. What had Plavgar said?

"We rejoice for her, and we are thankful to Mewenta."

Mewenta? But the husband of Lerrie was named Rownar. Who was Mewenta, and what did he have to do with the coming birth of Lerrie's child?

Canady snapped his fingers. Of course! He knew who Mewenta had to be, and that meant—

He got to his feet, the blood racing in his veins. He hurried outside into the twilight shadows. He knew the question now. It was time to get an answer.

Canady soon found that it was easier to determine upon a course of action than to carry it out. He had worked over his data longer than he had thought and twilight was already deepening into night when he tried to find Plavgar for another conference.

He found him quickly enough but Plavgar was busy.

The hunters had all come in, loaded down with ye-doma meat, and smooth firm-fleshed fish had been taken from the mountain streams. The women had prepared the evening meal and built up the fires against the night. The People had gathered in knots around the fires and Canady saw at once that there was some kind of ceremony going on.

It was not the sort of thing that a man could interrupt gracefully. Canady stayed in the shadows and watched.

It was a curious ritual, a mixture of wild abandon and solemn, highly stylized movements that were as old as time and performed with an immemorial artistry. There was a definite rhythm to the ritual, but it was a rhythm of motion rather than of music; no instruments were used and the only sounds came from cadenced human voices.

The women sat in groups of four around the fires. In the center of the camp, dressed in a long blue tunic, Lerrie stood on a low platform of logs. Her skin gleamed like gold in the firelight and her long black hair glistened around her shoulders. She turned slowly on the platform, facing each group of women in turn. There was a happiness in her eyes that was good to see.

The men danced in a great circle around Lerrie, their deep voices chanting a song that was old when the very mountains were young. Every few minutes one man would detach himself from the circle and visit each of the woman-fires. At each fire he would raise his bare arms and address the women in a ritual speech. He would tell of the events of his life, taking care to mention the incidents he had shared with each woman, and then give an account of his personal exploits: coups he had counted on raiding parties, his moment of contact with his guardian spirit, stories of Long Walks and Old Ones. When he had completed the circle of the fires, he would choose one woman for his ceremonial mate and take her into the trees beside the mountain stream. After a time, the two of them would come back to the fires, the woman would seat herself in her group of four, and the man would resume his place in the circle. As far as Canady could determine, the only rule was that a man could not choose his own wife.

Canady watched in silence, feeling far more than a scientific interest in the proceedings. He felt desperately

alone, desperately out of things, like a penniless child
with his face pressed tight against the cold window of
a toy shop. He stood in the shadows of the firelight,
half in darkness and half in light, and he chewed on the
stem of his pipe with a longing and bitterness that
racked his soul. The stars were frozen above him, the
night was chill, and he had been long without a woman. . . .

The tireless chant continued and The People filled
the darkness with their rejoicing. Only Lerrie was
alone, and no man touched her. She stood smiling on
the log platform, radiantly lovely with the new life that
was stirring within her. Canady felt a strange kinship
with her, the kinship of the outsiders, but he re-
sented her too. She was the center of everything, and
he simply did not count.

He shook his head. This was a hell of a time for self-
pity.

He waited until dawn streaked the sky with gray,
waited until he could sense the great red sun hovering
beneath the mountain horizon. When the ceremony
was over and The People were laughing and talking
together in normal voices, he sought out Plavgar.

Plavgar smiled and touched his shoulder with something like pity. "Welcome, my son. I thank you for
your courtesy in waiting. It has been a long night for
you."

Canady nodded. "The longest of my life, I think.
May I ask you one more question, Plavgar?"

"We have no secrets, my son."

"You told me earlier that you rejoiced for Lerrie,
and that you were thankful to Mewenta. Who is Mewenta?"

Canady tensed. He knew the answer to the question
but he had to ask, had to be *sure*. He listened to Plavgar's words with a thrill of confirmation.

"Mewenta was a great man of The People. On the
night before you came to visit us, Ar-thur, he did a
wonderful thing for The People. He walked into the
fire and his spirit now lives here in the mountains.

Because of his deed, the Old Ones smiled. That is why Lerrie now will have a child."

Canady remembered that night. They had hidden in a clump of bushes, looking down on a scene of wild magnificence. A thousand natives had gathered around a roaring fire and the tepees had shone in the moonlight. A naked man bowed to the four directions, gave a last farewell look out into the night and the moons and the stars. His face had been supremely peaceful, the face of a man who had reached the end of a long, long journey.

He walked into the roaring flames. . . .

Mewenta.

Canady turned and walked back to the sphere. He should have been tired but nothing was further from his mind than sleep. He felt an electric excitement in his muscles, an almost supernatural clearness in his mind.

He shook Frank's shoulder.

"Frank, wake up."

Frank sat up in bed, rubbing his eyes. "What's the matter? What time is it?"

"Frank, I've got it. I know about The People now."

Frank Landis groped for a cigarette, eyeing his companion sleepily. "Know about The People? What is there to know?"

Canady laughed. "God, and we tried to impress them with sewing machines!"

Frank waited, puffing on his cigarette. "Well?"

"Frank, don't you see? We've walked right smack into the middle of the biggest discovery ever made by man. Frank, The People *don't die*."

"What?"

"They don't die, at least not naturally. They're immortal, Frank. They live forever."

Frank stared at him, the cigarette forgotten in his hand.

"Immortal," Canady said again.

He walked over to the port and looked out at the red splendor of the morning sun.

IV

Two hours later, while the camp slept around them and the warmth of the day inched up toward the mountain snows, the men from Earth were still at it. The sphere was blue with stale tobacco smoke and the coffee dregs had turned gummy in the cups.

"I did *not* say you were crazy, Arthur," Frank said. "That's not fair."

Canady watched him and had to smile. Despite the words that tumbled from his lips, Frank obviously thought he was trapped with a lunatic—or at best with a man on the edge of sanity. And Canady was finding it very difficult to *talk* to Frank. Frank's eager, friendly personality and his guileless blue eyes just didn't belong in the same room with talk about immortality. It was like trying to explain to a three-year-old child that the Earth wasn't *really* flat but only looked that way.

"It's true, Frank. Our opinions won't change it any."

"But look." Frank nodded his head up and down solemnly, determined to explode the fallacies in the argument. "It just doesn't stand to reason. You say these natives live practically forever. OK. That means that they are maybe thousands of years old. Think what a man could learn if he lived to be a thousand years old! Dammit, he wouldn't be living like a savage. He would have developed a superior, advanced kind of culture. Isn't that true?"

Canady stoked up his pipe. He was feeling lightheaded from the long hours without sleep. But if he could just make Frank see—

"I agree. He wouldn't be living like a savage. And he would live in a very advanced type of culture."

Frank threw up his hands. "Well?"

"Well what?" Canady leaned forward. "Think a minute. Are The People *really* living like savages, and what the devil does that mean anyhow? Do you mean they are savages because they hunt animals for food?

Or because they live in tents instead of skyscrapers? Or because they use bows and arrows instead of rifles or atom bombs?"

"But their technology *is* simple. You can't deny that."

"I don't have to deny it. Just the same, simple isn't savage. After all, what's a technology for? How do you judge it? I would think you have to rate it by seeing what it does in terms of its own cultural context. The only real index of technological advancement is one of relative efficiency. What do you want a rifle for if you don't need one? What do you need a doctor for if you never get sick?"

"It isn't an efficient technology. You can't tell me a bow is more efficient than a rifle for a hunter. It *isn't*."

"It is in a special situation, and this is one of them. Look, it's obvious that for some reason these societies must be kept small. Not only that, but they must be peaceful. If they've hit a perfect balance in ecological terms with a bow and arrow, a rifle would just foul everything up. The one cardinal fact about an immortal society is that it must survive. If it doesn't, it's not immortal. And therefore anything that *in the long run* does not contribute to survival cannot be tolerated. Hell, you can't argue with the thing. It *works*."

"All right, all right." Frank poured himself another cup of coffee. "But all that is theory, speculation. It doesn't prove that those natives live forever."

"True enough. But try this on for size: there is not a single child in this village. There is not a single elderly person. The People can hardly remember when they were young, it was so long ago. And until Mewenta chose to destroy himself, Lerrie could not have a child. When Mewenta died it was such a singular event that natives for miles around came into camp just to witness it. When Lerrie announced that she was pregnant, the whole tribe went into a delirium of joy. It can only mean one thing: this is a rigidly controlled population. No child can be born until the death of an adult makes room for a new member of the society. It would *have* to work that way. If nobody dies and children keep on being born The People would breed themselves into extinction."

"I'll go along with that up to a point. I think you have demonstrated that we have a rigidly controlled population here. I admit that I've never heard of anything like it. But that still doesn't prove all this immortality stuff."

Canady sighed. He was talking to a stone wall. "Look, Frank. *Why* didn't The People accept those sewing machines and rifles? *Why* weren't they impressed with that bomb we dropped, or with this sphere for that matter? *Why* have we failed to make the slightest impression on them?"

"You said it yourself. If you destroy a perfect ecological adjustment . . ." Frank stopped.

"Exactly. *But how do they know that?* Who told them about ecological adjustments? How could they possibly know what effect a rifle will have on their culture? You started out by saying they were a bunch of savages. Now you're saying they know all about the effects of acculturation and cultural dynamics. You can't have it both ways."

Frank lapsed into silence.

"It's more than just ecology, Frank. I'm convinced that this immortality angle is *part* of their culture— a product of it. It isn't a mutant gland or a shot of wonder drug in the gizzard. It comes about *because* they live the way they do. They know that. So of course they're not going to jeopardize it by changing their culture. What's a rifle or a spaceship against the prospects of living forever? Think of it, Frank! No lying awake nights wondering if that ache in your belly is cancer. No sitting in a hospital room wondering if your wife will live until morning. No certain knowledge that you will see your father and mother buried in a hole in the ground. No waiting for your muscles to turn flabby and the saliva to drool from the corners of your mouth when you eat. No watching a friend get skinnier day by day, no watching the light go out of his eyes. My God, would you trade that for a sewing machine?"

Frank shook his head. "I always read that if you lived forever you would be unhappy and bored stiff. How about that?"

Canady laughed. "Man, that is the rationalization of the ages. You can't live forever, therefore you don't want to. You can't have a steak, therefore you aren't hungry. Are The People unhappy? I'd say they're a million times happier than most men and women on Earth. And would you *really* fight against it if you knew you could live forever? I wouldn't! My life hasn't been any screaming ecstasy but I'll hang onto it as long as I can. And if I could live forever, if I could really do the things I love—"

How do you speak of these things to another? How do you tell of blue skies and sunlight and the laughter of love? How do you tell the joys of just being alive, of knowing that the world of winds and trees and mountain streams is yours to cherish forever? How do you tell of a love that endures for all the years, all the springs?

"Mewenta killed himself," Frank said bluntly.

"Sure, not all people are happy, and these natives *are* people. And perhaps a man might even sacrifice eternal life to bring joy to his fellow man, the joy of children. I have heard that when a man of The People feels restless or discontented, he sets out on a Long Walk alone. He gets close to the land to cleanse his heart. It usually works. If not, there's always the fire."

"You spoke of peace. How about all this raiding that goes on?"

"You mean counting coups?" Canady shrugged. "Sure, they go off and rustle the mharu herds. They have real knock-down fights too. But who said a culture like this has to be dull? It *couldn't* be dull. They don't kill each other in the fights. Have you noticed the combs the men wear in their hair? That's what they take instead of scalps. It serves the same purpose. You don't kill a guy in a football game either, but you can get plenty steamed up about it. *Everything* in the culture is set up to avoid boredom. They alternate roles, for one thing. Every five years or so everyone switches positions. Plavgar is the headman now, but that is only one of the many parts he has played in his life. And all the ceremonies, the periods when the sex tabus are lifted—they all serve the same purpose. Dammit, The People like to have *fun*."

Frank lit another cigarette. "If it's true, Arthur—we've got to find out how it's done. We've *got* to."

Canady smiled. "Have The People ever lied to us?"

"No, I guess not."

"How do they say it's done?"

"I don't follow you."

Canady got up, stretched, and yawned. "I think you better brush up on your guardian spirits, Frank. I think you better start thinking about the Old Ones."

Frank stared. "But that's all superstition—"

"Is it? *How do you know?* Have you ever fasted on Thunder Rock?"

Canady turned before Frank could answer him. He peeled off his clothes and fell into his bunk. He closed his tired eyes.

And he thought—

The world of winds and trees and mountain streams yours to cherish forever . . .

V

The days flowed into weeks and the weeks became months. The People drifted south along the sheltered slopes of the blue mountain range and the cold winter snows settled on the grasslands in a blanket of white. Only the brown and black tips of the grasses showed above the rolling sea of snow and the yedoma herds turned their backs to the wind and pawed at the frozen soil with cold and bleeding hooves.

Arthur Canady lived as though in a dream. He was not himself and he felt the very foundations of the world he had known crumbling away beneath him. Subtly, without any clear line of transition, he found himself caught between two different ways of life. He lived in a cultural twilight, an outsider, belonging neither to the world of his past nor to the world that had suddenly opened up before him.

I'm a marginal man, he thought. *Me, Arthur Canady, a scientist. I don't fit anywhere. Maybe I've never fit in, not really. Maybe I've been searching all my life, never finding, never knowing what it was I sought . . .*

He spent part of his time in the sphere with Frank, surrounded by the familiar gadgets he had always known, both attracted and repelled by the personality of his companion. The man was such a mixture of receptiveness and bull-headedness. Like most naïve men, Frank prided himself on being utterly practical. He was tolerant and respectful of new ideas, but he could never change beyond a certain point. His personality was a finished thing; it had nowhere else to go. Canady envied him in a way, but he was unable to communicate with him except on a very superficial level.

He spent part of his time with The People, riding with them on the winter-thin mharus, facing the wind-driven snows with Plavgar and Lerrie and Rownar. He learned to bring down the moose-like yedoma bulls with an arrow behind the left shoulder, learned to cut the blood-warm hides from the bodies with a stone knife, learned to drink the hot blood against the cold of the winter plains. He sat in the smoke-hazed tepees at night, sweating with the others around the tiny fires of yedoma chips, listening to the stories of The People.

Still, he did not belong.

The People smiled at him and seemed glad to see him, but there was a barrier he could not cross. The men were friendly without being his friends, the women cordial but invincibly remote. Canady let his hair and beard grow long and began to dress in the skin clothing of the natives. There were many times when he set out across the plains alone, eyes narrowed against the cold, and there were many nights that he looked up at the frozen stars and wondered which one was the sun he had known on Earth. . . .

And the dark, terrible irony of the thing that was happening gnawed at his mind day and night. He would sit and smoke his pipe, staring at Frank. Didn't he *know*?

Canady had always been a lonely man, lonely not only for companionship but for richness and a fullness he had never found in life. His loneliness was made doubly unbearable by the vitality of the life around him. The People offered him nothing, denied him nothing. They made no overtures. They were simply there.

And life everlasting . . .

Canady abandoned all pretense of scientific investigation. He went to see Plavgar. He seated himself in the tepee on Plavgar's right, ate of the ritual food, and groped for words.

"The Old Ones were here before The People came," he said, thinking like a native. But his mind refused to stay on that level. He thought: *Everything they have told me has been the literal truth. There* are *Old Ones. What are they? In the vastness of the universe, life must take many forms. Do they coexist with men, manifesting themselves only in visions? Could they have existed on Earth, serving as the basis for primitive legends? Who knows what we destroyed when we sailed into strange harbors with our ships and our diseases? We never saw our natives until we had corrupted them.* "They must be powerful beings. Did they not try to defend their world?"

"Conquest is a delusion of the young, my son," Plavgar said slowly. "There is room for all. The lives of the Old Ones and the lives of The People touch in only a few places. We are equal but different. To them, as to us, harmony is the highest law of the universe. We all must live so that we *blend* with one another. Men and Old Ones and plants and birds and animals and sky and water—all must work together to make a world fair and good. The Old Ones have

given life to us. In return, we give them happiness.
They can *feel* the warmth of our lives. They need our
presence, just as we need theirs. We live together, and
we are both the better for it."

Canady leaned forward. "You too once came to
this world in ships?"

Plavgar smiled. "It was long ago. Yes, once we were
civilized and advanced, just like yourself."

The irony of the headman's words was not lost on
Canady. He brushed it aside. "Plavgar, what is the
secret? What is the price a man must pay for eternal
life?"

Plavgar looked at him steadily. "We do not live forever, my son. A very long time, yes, but not forever."

"But there must be a secret! What is it?"

"There is only one rule. *You must learn to have a
good heart.*"

Canady swallowed hard. "A good heart?"

"That is all. I have told you the truth. I have con-
cealed nothing from you. We have no secrets. There is
no magic pill, no gadget that will bring you what you
seek. You must *believe,* that is all. You must have a
good heart."

"But—" Canady's mind was dizzy with what Plavgar
was saying. A good heart? He had learned many things
in many schools, but no one had taught him this. How
did a man go about getting a good heart?

"A man's heart is within himself," Plavgar said
simply. "You must look around you, at the mountains
and the skies, at the plants and the animals. You must
look within yourself. You must feel that you are a
part of all life, and respect it. You must find peace.
Then you must go to Thunder Rock and fast for four
days. And if you believe, if your heart is good, you
will see the Old Ones. The guardian spirit will come to
you. Then, my son, you will be one of The People—
for always."

The yedoma-chip fire flickered brightly in the tepee.
The shadows closed in around Canady, shadows and
something else . . .

"Thank you, Plavgar," he said.

He got up and left the tepee, walking out into the cold night air. His boots crunched the snow under his feet.

All he had to do was to believe. All he had to do was to reject all he had ever known. All he had to do was to get a good heart.

Simple!

And there were other problems, other loyalties.

He walked back alone to the sphere.

When he told Frank what he was going to do, Frank hit the ceiling.

"You can't do it, Art." Frank's face was very pale. He backed away from his bearded, wild-looking companion as though Canady was a carrier of some frightful disease. "It's against the law."

"Whose law? We're a long way from Earth, my friend. I'm not a soldier. I'm a scientist."

"You're a fool! Dammit, can't you see what you're doing? You've got a wild bee in your brain and all that talk about being a scientist is so much hogwash. You're going native! You, Arthur Canady, hot-shot scientist!"

"All right. I'm going native."

"Look, Art. It's more than that. It's—it's disloyal, that's what it is. You can't just turn your back on your own people for a bunch of wild hunters."

"I can try."

Frank's anger got the better of his caution. "You act like you're so damned superior to everyone, you and your sarcasm! And look at you! What the hell is a good heart? You'll park yourself up on the mountain and starve to death waiting for some native gods to come and hand you immortality. It's crazy, Art! I won't let you do it."

Canady smiled. He stood there, tall and lean and toughened by his life on the plains. His green eyes were cold. "You can't stop me, Frank. Don't try."

"Forget about me. How about your own people, your friends? Don't you owe them something? You're al-

ways spouting off about ethics, but what are you doing? You're a traitor!"

Canady sighed. "You still don't see it, do you?"

"See what? There's nothing to see."

"Yes, there *is* something to see. You spoke of ethics.
Have you ever heard a phrase about doing to others
as you would have them do unto you? I suggest you
think about it a little."

"What are you talking about?"

"Look, Frank. We came here from Earth with a
lot of high-sounding notions about helping the natives,
didn't we? What was it that we offered them, essen-
tially? We offered them what we thought was progress
for a price. We would give them technological advance-
ments if they would simply agree to change their culture, their way of life. All they had to do was learn to
live the way we do and we would give them something
of what we had. Of course, we didn't put the offer to
them honestly. We tried to trick them into it—all from
the very highest motives, naturally. Was that ethical?"

Frank shrugged. "You tell me."

"I am telling you. If it was ethical, then you can't
damn the natives for giving us a dose of our own
morals. If it wasn't ethical, then it's pointless for us
to prattle about right and wrong. Don't you see, Frank?
They've turned the tables on us. They're offering us
exactly what we offered to them. The joker is that
they seem to have the superior culture, if that adjec-
tive means anything. They'll give us what they have:
eternal life. And the price we have to pay is the same
price we were going to charge them: all we have to do
is change our culture and live the way *they* do. It's
beautiful and neat and maybe a little frightening. But
at least they were honest about it: no tricks, no high-
pressure salesmanship. The choice is there. What we
do with it is up to us."

"It's fantastic! You can't believe—"

"I've *got* to believe. That's the whole point. And
don't make the mistake of underestimating these natives. They are far from helpless. They have the best

of all defenses: a good offense. They protect themselves by *giving*. We could destroy their culture, sure. But if we do we throw away our only chance for immortality! We *need* their culture. Oh, they're safe enough."

"Art, even if you believe all that stuff you still have a duty to your own people. You signed on to do a job. You can't just walk out on it."

"I'm not going to walk out on it. That's why I came back here. I'm going to write up precisely what I have discovered, leaving out nothing. There will be no secrets. I am going to tell our own people exactly what I have found. Hell, I'm giving them the secret of practically eternal life! What man ever did more for his people? If they don't believe me, that's their business. I'm giving them the chance. And I'm giving them the key that may one day unlock this culture, if they will only use it. You see, we made our big mistake in trying to impress The People with technological gadgets. They just don't *care* about technology. Perhaps if we had tried something else—Shakespeare, poetry, art, music—they might have listened to us. I don't know."

Frank shook his head. "You need a doctor."

Canady smiled. "Not any more, pal. And I'll tell you something else. I hope everyone *does* think I'm cracked. I hope they dismiss my report and toss it in the trash file. My conscience is clear. I've found what I want. All I want now is to be let alone."

"You're really going?"

Canady walked over and sat down at his desk. "I'm going to write this report. It will take a couple of days. After that, I'm going out alone."

"To get a good heart?"

"To get a good heart."

Canady assembled his notes and went to work.

Frank Landis stared at him and ran his hand through his sandy hair. Almost desperately, he picked up two battery-powered sewing machines and went out into the snow to peddle his wares.

VI

The lakes and ponds were still frozen solid and the mountain streams were still glazed with ice. The barren black brush of the plains was still skeletal and gaunt against the drifts of silver snow and the winter winds still whined down the canyons and froze the sweat on your face into little drops and rivulets of ice.

Yet the worst was over when Arthur Canady left the sphere and the camp of The People and set out alone into the wilderness. The snow-choked blizzards and the rivers of knife-edged winds had passed. The winter was resting, holding its own, waiting for the spring thaws and the return of green to the land. The gray winter skies had turned to cloudless blue and the great red sun was warm again on his back.

You must feel that you are part of all life. . . .

It was a strange Odyssey and Canady felt that strangeness keenly. It was a quest for the intangible, a search for the unknown. Canady was a trained man and he felt competent to search for many things: success in a field he knew, material prosperity, the solution to a scientific problem. He was enough of a product of his culture to feel at home looking for gold or uranium or a prize set of horns to hang over an old-fashioned fireplace.

But a good heart?

That wasn't so easy. Where did you look? How did you go about it? His scientific training got in his way. What was a good heart? It was a phrase he would have denounced as meaningless in a seminar discussion. It was mysticism. It was something for philosophers and theologians and politicians to kick around. It was fuzzy, slippery. . . .

You must look within yourself.

He rode out across the white-coated plains, drifting with the yedoma herds that offered him meat and warm furs. He watched the tiny tracks that crisscrossed over the crust of the snow. He watched the great birds that soared high in the sky on motionless, splendid wings. At night he pitched his small tent in whatever shelter he could find. He sat before his tiny fire and watched the twin moons float down the cold arc of the stars.

He rode into the far mountains, climbed the ageless rocks and stood with his head in the sky looking down upon the vastness of the land below him. He listened to the wind, rode through the whispers of the trees.

You must believe, that is all.

Perhaps he had help; he did not know. The Old Ones lived still in the high places, and perhaps they looked upon him with compassion. Canady felt a great peace growing within him, a peace he had never known in the cities of Earth. It was a hard life but he too became hard. He took a secret pleasure in the toughness of his body, in the sharpness of his eyes. He awakened with the sun, grateful for the life in his body, eager to see what the day would bring. Smiles came easily to his face and he was relaxed, free from worry.

Why had his people thrown all their energies into bigger buildings, more powerful ships, more intricate engines? Why did his people spend all of their lives grubbing at jobs they detested, their greatest joys coming from a slickly gutless mediocrity on the tri-di set? What had they mistaken for progress, what had they sacrificed to that strange god? How had it come about that pleasure had become something to snatch on the run, between business appointments, between the soggy oblivion of sleeping pills?

Progress.

Could it be that true progress might be found on a simple pathway through the trees and not on a super-freeway at all? Could it be that eternal life had always come from a kind of faith, from being close to the land and the world of living things?

If you believe, if your heart is good, you will see the Old Ones. The guardian spirit will come to you. Then, my son, you will be one of The People—for always.

Canady rode alone across the rolling plains and up twisting mountain trails. Winter lost its grip on the land and the streams leaped from their banks, fed by the melting snows. Patches of green came again to the lowland valleys and the first wildflowers poked up their heads toward the sun.

When he thought he was ready, Canady turned and rode high into the mountains. The warm spring wind brushed at his face and he filled his lungs with it in a kind of ecstasy. He was at peace, with himself and with the world around him. If nothing else, he had found that much.

He rode toward Thunder Rock to begin his fast.

Thunder Rock thrust its dark, wind-scarred bulk up into the sky high above the timber line where the last stunted trees clung to their precarious holds on the face of the mountain. There was a small cave in the side of Thunder Rock, a cave that opened upon a level sheet of stone that extended to the sheer face of a black glass-smooth cliff. Standing on that shelf of stone, a man could look down on the rivers of clouds that wound around the lower peaks.

Canady had tethered his mharu far down in a mountain valley where there was plenty of grass and water. He could see the valley from Thunder Rock, and once in a while he caught a glimpse of his mount, little more than a black dot on a stamp of green far below.

He allowed himself a few swallows of icy water from a nearby snowbank and that was all. He ate nothing. In the daylight hours he stood on the shelf of rock and looked down on the world, and at night he shivered in his cave. He had his fur robes but there was no material with which to make a fire.

The air was thin and seared his lungs. His joints were sore and stiff. The days without food left him weak and giddy, and he looked down at the black dot of the mharu and wondered whether he would ever be able to climb down the mountain again. He was surprised to find that his mind lost none of its sharpness.

In fact, it worked with an almost preternatural clarity, as though all problems were easy and all questions could be answered. He felt as though he were running a fever and he was reminded of the sensation of heightened awareness that sometimes comes with fever dreams. And then he remembered that when the fever was gone a man would wake up and everything that had seemed so clear would vanish like bubbles on the wind. . . .

The days and nights blurred together. He lay quietly in his cave and he had never felt less alone. It gave him an eerie sensation to think that each man and woman of The People had once slept where he was sleeping, walked where he was walking, thought where he was thinking. There was no visible sign that they had ever been here but he could see memories of them in every stone, in every stain of dampness, in every tongue of sunlight that licked at the cold surfaces of the rocks. He sensed a continuity of life that he had never appreciated before, a linking together of living things in an endless procession over the plains and into the wild mountain ranges.

On the fourth night, the rains came.

A sea of swollen clouds washed over the stars. For long minutes the moonlight gleamed on the edges of the clouds, setting them aflame with pink and silver light, and then the darkness was complete. There was an electric hush as the world held its breath.

Then the lightning came, jagged white forks of frozen fire that flashed down from black cloud masses and hurled themselves with livid fury at the stolid bulk of the mountains. The thunder crashed on the heels of the lightning, splitting through the skies with a tearing, ripping explosiveness that tore the very air apart.

Canady huddled in his cave, blinking at the savagery of the storm. The walls of the cave were white with the continuous flashing of the lightning, his ears roared with the brute power of the thunder.

Thunder Rock!

The rain came down in solid sheets, hissing on the ledge of stone, pouring in torrents down the cracks and crevices of the mountains. The stone shelf outside the cave became a puddle, a lake, and the water washed into the cave itself, soaking his feet.

Canady stood up, his head almost touching the roof of the cave. He did not fear the storm. He ignored the water at his feet. He stared out into the raging night.

The guardian spirit will come to you.

His skin crawled. A prickling sensation ran up and down his spine. He narrowed his eyes, tried to see. The white flashes of the lightning were everywhere. The thunder beat at his ears.

He *felt* them. He felt them all around him. He closed his eyes. There! He could almost see them—

The Old Ones.

Mighty, powerful, old when the mountains were young. And yet friendly, respectful, equals—

Canady clenched his fists.

He whispered the hardest prayer of all: "Let me believe! Oh, let me believe!"

There was a long moment when nothing seemed to happen. Then, abruptly, the lightning and the thunder died away. The storm rolled off into the distance, muttering and grumbling to itself. There was silence except for the soft patter of the rain outside the cave.

Canady opened his eyes. There was a sinking sensation in his chest. Had he failed? Was it all for nothing?

Then he saw it.

A great bird flew out of the darkness and perched on the rain-wet shelf of rock. He looked like a hawk, an eagle. He was a mighty bird, raven-black, bold eyes glittering in his head, great wings folded at his sides. There was nothing supernatural about him. Canady could see the drops of water on his feathers, hear the faint whistle when he breathed.

And yet—

The guardian spirit will come to you.

The eagle walked toward the cave.

Canady stepped forward to meet it.

Suddenly, the cave was alive. He saw them now, all around him, glowing like creatures of light and energy.

They touched him and they were warm. They seemed to have faces and they were smiling, smiling. . . .

Canady felt tears in his eyes, tears neither of happiness nor of sorrow, tears that came from an emotion too strong to be borne, too mighty to be named. He stood up straight as a man stands among his friends.

And the night was dark no longer and the stars looked down on him from a bright and peaceful sky.

VII

The small gray metallic sphere lifted from the camp of The People but now it carried one man instead of two. It gleamed dully in the light from the great red sun. It hovered high above the surface of Pollux V, looking down on a world flushed with green. It paced the planet as the world rotated on its axis.

It seemed a puny thing as it awaited the arrival of the mother ship from the CAS fleet of Earth, dwarfed by the vault of the heavens and the vast expanse of the land below it. One day it might return, but there were easier worlds for contact. And hidden in its tapes and papers and records it carried a secret no man would believe, a key that could have unlocked one of the hidden secrets of the universe.

Frank Landis sat on his bunk, surrounded by his sewing machines and rifles and model steam engines. He fingered them each in turn, his blue eyes blank and staring, thinking about the crazy man he had left behind. . . .

And the man who had been Arthur Canady came down from Thunder Rock and rode out of the mountains onto the wind-swept plains. The land was green with the promise of spring, the promise of world renewal, the promise of budding trees and fresh grasses and air so clean you could taste it.

His every sense was heightened, he was alive as he had never been alive before. His heart was a song within him. He knew that the wife of the great Me-

wenta would be stolen by the Telliomata to make
room for him, and he knew that this was a good thing,
a happy thing.

The ship was not going home. *He* was going home.

And when he rode into the village of The People
there was a smile on every face, and there was a new
tepee in the camp circle.

And Plavgar came to meet him and raised his arms
in welcome.

And the Old Ones who walked at his side forever
whispered to him as he rode, whispered down the
winds and across the fields, whispered down from the
free skies where the eagle flew, whispered to him
alone—

"Welcome, brother, welcome."

SCIENCE FICTION AND FANTASY INDEX

BOOKS:
Mists of Dawn, John C. Winston Co., 1952 (novel).
Shadows in the Sun, Ballantine Books, 1954 (novel).
Another Kind, Ballantine Books, 1955 (collection).
The Winds of Time, Doubleday, 1957 (novel).
Unearthly Neighbors, Ballantine Books, 1960 (novel).

IN MAGAZINES:

1950
"The Land of Lost Content," *Super Science Stories*, November.

1951
"The Blood Star" (with Garvin Berry), *Super Science Stories*, January.
"The Boy Next Door," *Fantasy and Science Fiction*, June.
"The Reporter," *Fantastic Story Magazine*, Fall.
"The Edge of Forever," *Astounding Science Fiction*, December.

1952
"The Subversives," *Startling Stories*, February.
"Lady Killer," *Startling Stories*, March.
"Blood's a Rover," *Astounding Science Fiction*, May.
"Stardust," *Astounding Science Fiction*, July.
"The Fires of Forever," *Science Fiction Adventures*, November.
"Final Exam," *Fantastic*, December.

1953
"Technical Adviser," *Fantasy and Science Fiction*, February.
"Judgment Day," *Science Fiction Adventures*, March.
"The Shore of Tomorrow," *Startling Stories*, March.
"Anachronism," *Fantasy and Science Fiction*, April.
"The Ant and the Eye," *Astounding Science Fiction*, April.
"Hardly Worth Mentioning," *Fantastic*, May-June.
"The Life Game," *Thrilling Wonder Stories*, June.
"Hands Across Space," *Science Fiction Plus*, August.

1954
"Let Me Live in a House," *Universe Science Fiction*, March.

"Rite of Passage," *Astounding Science Fiction*, April.

"Of Course," *Astounding Science Fiction*, May.

"Controlled Experiment," *Orbit Science Fiction*, Issue 5, November–December.

"Transformer," *Fantasy and Science Fiction*, November.

1955

"Field Experiment," *Astounding Science Fiction*, January.

"Night," *If*, March.

"The Last Word" (with Charles Beaumont), *Fantasy and Science Fiction*, April.

"Artifact," *Fantasy and Science Fiction*, June.

"Any More at Home Like You?" original for *Star Science Fiction # 3*, Ballantine.

"The Mother of Necessity," "A Star Above It," originals for *Another Kind*, Ballantine.

1956

"I, Claude" (with Charles Beaumont), *Fantasy and Science Fiction*, February.

"North Wind," *Fantasy and Science Fiction*, March.

"The Guests of Chance" (with Charles Beaumont), *Infinity*, June.

1957

"Didn't He Ramble," *Fantasy and Science Fiction*, April.

"Between the Thunder and the Sun," *Fantasy and Science Fiction*, May.

"The Wind Blows Free," *Fantasy and Science Fiction*, July.

"Rewrite Man," *Fantasy and Science Fiction*, September.

1958

"Pilgrimage," *Fantasy and Science Fiction*, February.

"The Space Horde," *Amazing*, February.

"Guardian Spirit," ("The Marginal Man"), *Fantasy and Science Fiction*, April.

1959

"From Little Acorns," *Satellite Science Fiction*, February.

"The One That Got Away," *Fantasy and Science Fiction*, May.

"Transfusion," *Astounding Science Fiction*, June.

1965

"End of the Line," *Fantasy and Science Fiction*, January.

"A Stick for Harry Eddington," *Fantasy and Science Fiction*, August.

1966

"Just Like a Man," *Fantastic*, July.